Emily Prager
EVE'S TATTOO

Emily Prager is the author of *A Visit from the Footbinder* and *Clea and Zeus Divorce*. She writes a regular column for *Penthouse* and lives in New York City. *Eve's Tattoo* was a finalist for the 1991 National Jewish Book Award.

ALSO BY *Emily Prager*

Clea and Zeus Divorce
A Visit from the Footbinder
World War II Resistance Stories

EVE'S TATTOO

EVE'S TATTOO

Emily Prager

Vintage Contemporaries

VINTAGE BOOKS

A DIVISION OF RANDOM HOUSE, INC.

NEW YORK

FIRST VINTAGE CONTEMPORARIES EDITION, NOVEMBER 1992

Copyright © 1991 by Emily Prager

All rights reserved under International and Pan-American Copyright Conventions. Published in the United States by Vintage Books, a division of Random House, Inc., New York, and simultaneously in Canada by Random House of Canada Limited, Toronto. Originally published in hardcover by Random House, Inc., New York, in 1991.

Library of Congress Cataloging-in-Publication Data
Prager, Emily.
Eve's tattoo / Emily Prager. — 1st Vintage Contemporaries ed.
p.   cm.
Originally published: New York: Random House, 1991.
ISBN 0-679-74053-8 (pbk.)
I. Title.
[PS3566.R25E95   1992]
813'.54—dc20   92-50072
CIP

Author photograph © Ron Rinaldi

Manufactured in the United States of America
10   9   8   7   6   5   4   3   2   1

For the women who resist,
and the women who don't

Germany is my bride.
—Adolf Hitler

I am deeply indebted to the many authors and editors of the histories, witness accounts, and original source materials concerning the Third Reich that I've used as references. In particular, to Claudia Koontz, author of *Mothers in the Fatherland;* Robert N. Proctor, author of *Racial Hygiene;* and J. Noakes and G. Pridham, editors of *Nazism,* volumes 1 and 2. Without the historical details, facts, and incidents that I found within their books, Eva's tales could not have been imagined.

My sincere thanks for their intellectual support and encouragement to Christian Rohr, Steven Marcus, Peter Foges, Lynn Philips, Frank McHugh, Sal Giglio, and the Penguin Cafe, Gary Lucas, Gully Wells, Francine Stasium, Arthur Prager, Nora Elcar, Jonathan Burnam, Carmen Callil, J. W. Johnson, and of course to my editor, Bob Loomis.

EVE'S TATTOO

I

Eve moved hesitantly down the unfamiliar street looking for number 27, Big Dan's Tattoo Parlor. It was hot, and the sun cast a bright yellow light that did nothing for the drab upstate town but lay bare its grimness. She seemed to be in an industrial section with square, two-story, flat-top buildings dating from the fifties and, in between them, the occasional dark, dank takeout. Across the street, three black kids loitered in front of a run-down launderette. Eve glanced nervously at them but they took no notice of her. She proceeded on, peering at the numbers, until she reached the glass door that read 27. She pulled it open and hurried inside up a long flight of stairs to her appointment.

To the left of the landing was Big Dan's Tattoo Parlor. She had found it in the Yellow Pages listed under "Tattoo." She had chosen it for its proximity to Manhattan. She had expected a place with a nautical motif, but when she crossed the doorsill she smiled at her misplaced fantasy. A screaming bell was triggered by her next footstep, and she jumped and turned and saw, quite close to her, a man seated at a beat-up desk by a telephone. A large, broken-looking biker guy with a kindly grin and tattooed arms, he nodded to her and she asked quickly, "Big Dan?"

"Nope," he replied.

"I have an appointment," she said, recovering her composure.

He nodded again. "Be here soon," he said pleasantly.

"Thanks," she said, nodding back. "I'll look around."

And with a faint, nervous smile, she walked past him into the interior.

It was a biker's den, a clubhouse for Hell's Angels, and it was crammed with oddities. On three walls were Scotch-taped hundreds of illustrations of the tattoos Big Dan offered: skulls with fire flaring from the eye sockets, swastikas festooned with roses, panthers on the attack, hearts with blanks for cherished names, snakes and dragons, mermaids and madwomen. There was a sign, too: WE COPY YOUR DESIGN. She patted her shoulder bag as if to confirm it.

Beneath the tattoos, chaotically arranged, were two murky, slime-filled fish tanks, an old TV, and a lopsided club chair that was ripped and oozed stuffing. Behind the chair stood an army-issue metal cabinet on top of which was a stack of chipped motorcycle helmets and, next to them, two Nazi infantry helmets with bullet holes through the temples.

In the center of the loft, a small prefab room with glass windows had been constructed, inside which the tattooing was done. Eve walked over to it and peered in. Basically it was an office, but two barber chairs sat amid the clutter alongside two electric tattooing devices that resembled dentist's drills. Garish Polaroids of tattooed human body parts decorated one wall: pendulous breasts with flowers round the nipples, beefy arms with heraldic crests, bulbous behinds with butterflies, all ugly, terribly ugly, like photos of skin diseases in medical magazines.

"Does it hurt?"

Eve came around the corner of the prefab room and addressed the biker guy. He was staring at her with dumb surprise wondering, rather obviously, what a girl like her was doing in a place like this.

"Depends on where you get 'em," he said. "The underside of the arm hurts more, more tender."

"Really," she said. "That's interesting."

Taped on the wall behind the biker guy were articles about Big Dan from various magazines and newspapers. A far corner was devoted to a drug bust of Hell's Angels in the East Village, an event that had occurred several years before. The newspapers were yellowed and curling. They had been retaped up many times, an important monument in biker lore.

"How long does it take for the swelling to go down?" Eve asked.

"Oh . . . ," The biker guy mulled this over. "Three to five hours, depending. And you have to put bacitracin ointment on it. I put it on ten times a day 'cause I'm nervous."

He laughed sweetly to himself. He was, she thought, referring obliquely to AIDS, trying to reassure her.

"Do you worry about AIDS?" she asked as she walked toward a strange piece of taxidermy at the end of the room.

"Nope," he replied. "Disposable needles. Steam cleaning. And you get your own new pots of ink, then they throw them away. Nobody died yet."

"Good," said Eve but she wasn't fully listening. She was transfixed by the object before her.

It was a dusty display case, maybe four feet by two feet, containing five dirty-white, dried-out sea creatures with dragon heads, wings, and feet. A small, hand-typed paper under the glass proclaimed: "Devilfish. Rarely seen. Caught by Big Dan on the Orinoco after his party was wiped out by the headhunting Pinoa Indians."

"Devilfish," she said.

"Yeah," the biker guy nodded. "They're weird. Somethin' humanoid about 'em."

There was. Something about the froggy legs and feet, the rounded skulls. Like monstrous, ill-conceived fetuses.

There was a thunderous footfall. A bell screamed. And Eve snapped around just as a huge man in a biker outfit crossed the doorsill. He stopped and stared at her with suspicion.

"Big Dan?" she asked.

He didn't reply.

"I'm Eve. I phoned. I have an appointment."

He looked her up and down.

"You a writer?" he asked, sneering.

"Yes," Eve replied. "But that's not why I'm here. I've come to get a tattoo."

Big Dan shrugged.

"I'm an editor myself," he said. "I write a column."

Eve's heart was pounding.

"For what?" she ventured.

"*Outlaw Biker!*" He threw this down like a gauntlet.

"I've read *Easy Rider,*" she parried.

He spat on the floor with disgust.

"Piece of shit," he snarled.

The biker guy by the telephone winced. Eve smiled politely.

"Yes," she agreed. "Commercial."

Big Dan strode over to the fish tanks and switched on their lights. It seemed there was something living in there, something that Eve had missed. Then he moved to the prefab room, unlocked the door, and went inside.

Big Dan was, as his name indicated, a big grizzly of a man with overdeveloped tattooed arms, and a fat, splayed face that viewed the world with distaste. He stood about six-three, weighed in at two-eighty-five, was clean-shaven, and wore jeans and a black T-shirt and a frayed black leather vest. Eve watched him through the glass window as he lumbered about, readying one of the barber chairs for her appointment.

His tattoos were elaborate and violent. One arm was devoted to Vietnam. A C-130 flew on his bicep, below which, all along his forearm, rice paddies exploded with napalm, and coolie-hatted, black-pajamaed figures ran engulfed in flame. NAM was inked in blood red on the top of one hand and, coiled around the letters, a naked Vietnamese beauty lay fingering her long black hair.

The other arm featured Nazi Germany. On his bicep, the full insignia of the elite Totenkopf, or Death's-Head Squadron of the SS, was perfectly inked with its lightning bolts and skull, and then along the forearm, swastikas and iron crosses, ending on top of his hand with ACHTUNG, around which coiled a naked blonde with red lips and a rolled hairdo from the 1940s.

It interested Eve that though the Nazis earned glorification in the tattoo world, the Vietcong did not. It was a matter of style and dedication. All the pungee sticks and bamboo prisons in the world just couldn't come close to one white man's death camp.

Big Dan caught sight of Eve watching him and glared menacingly at her. She didn't care. She suddenly felt dizzy and nauseous and as if she could vomit up hundreds and thousands of celebrity names and anecdotes right there on the floor. One massive heave and up would come everything she had ever heard or read about Michael Jackson, Bianca Jagger, Princess Diana, Elizabeth Taylor. One massive heave and up would come the publishing world and Hollywood, the White House and the music business. One massive heave and up would come the art world and television and New York, and New York, and New York.

"Come on," Big Dan was calling her.

She walked into the prefab room and sat down on one of the barber chairs.

Big Dan was wary of this girl. She could be a reporter. She could be from the Health Department. He fiddled ostentatiously with a disposable needle and took his time inserting it into the mechanism. She was some kind of college girl, that much was clear, a little too fearless for his taste.

"So?" he snarled when he was ready.

"So," said Eve, "you said on the phone you'd copy my design?"

"I said 'maybe.' I have to see it. I'm not doin' any daisies. No fuckin' daisies!"

Eve opened the bag and pulled out a manila envelope. She opened it and said, "It's my birthday today. This is my birthday present to myself. I'm forty."

Big Dan looked shocked.

7

"Forty," he repeated, staring at her. "You don't look no forty. See that guy out there?" He pointed to the guy by the telephone. "That guy's thirty-three!"

Something was wrong here, very wrong. Big Dan drew back.

"I know I don't," Eve said, drawing a photo from the envelope. "That's part of the problem. Here—" She thrust the photo at Big Dan.

"It's very simple. Here's what I want. Just like this. Can you do this?"

Big Dan looked at the photo and then back at Eve. She was very pretty, round-faced and classy, in her summer dress, her white-blond hair so neatly cut. He peered into her childlike eyes and saw nothing there but innocence. That scared him.

"You can see it here, can't you?" Eve went on. "Six numbers facing outward, along the underside of the arm? Five-zero-zero-one-two-three. See how they're squiggly, done in a hurry, badly? That's just how I want them, not straight and well done like you would probably do them. Okay?"

She smiled at him entreatingly. Her smile was so sweet it made him cringe. He wanted her out of there as quickly as possible.

He opened a pot of blue-black ink, turned on the machine, and began the job. His hand was shaking. 5-0-0-1-2-3. He glanced often at the photo as he inked in the numbers. He looked up at her once and saw tears rolling down her cheeks.

When he was finished, she took a lace handkerchief from her purse and dried her face. Then, in silence, they left the prefab room and she paid him at the front desk.

"What'd she want?" the biker guy asked as she crossed the doorsill.

Big Dan did not reply until she traversed the landing and headed down the stairs.

"The I.D. numbers of a death camp victim. I tattooed 'em on the debutante's arm."

II

When Eve opened the door to their loft, Charles César was angry. He was on the phone speaking softly in French, but Eve could tell he was pissed. She knew it because she had lived with him for two years. There were no external signs. Charlie's was a stately kind of anger, as classy as the rest of him. He never raised his voice. He never sneered. He wore his anger, in his fortieth year, quietly and gracefully like a priest's cassock.

Eve loved Charles César. She gazed at him as he ran his small hand through his glossy black hair. He grinned at her between whispered tirades. He was about five foot ten and elegant in his movements. He was always dressed up. He always wore a tie. People thought he was a member of some royal family, a European or even Arab prince. Though he was French, he looked of indeterminate nationality, and Eve was mesmerized by the sight of him. She blew him a kiss, and fled down the hall to their bedroom.

The swelling on her arm had gone down a bit. The numbers were visible now, 500123, and the redness was fading. Eve sat down on the bed, took the bacitracin ointment from her purse, and rubbed it across the tattoo. It hurt like hell.

She slipped off her shoes and lay down. Six-thirty. They had an hour before they had to be at Cilla's party. Eve wanted to sleep but she couldn't, and after a while she dragged her purse across the coverlet, opened the manila envelope, and pulled from it the photograph.

It had been taken in 1944 at Auschwitz concentration camp, it said on the back. It was a close shot of three women standing in a line. They wore dresses and they still had their hair, but you could tell something awful was going on. Two of the women were hunched over, from cold or fear, their heads buried in their shoulders, actively avoiding the camera. The third stared aggressively at the lens, her back straight, her chin up, an evil little grimace of defiance on her pretty face. She held out one arm, underside turned up, so her fresh tattoo could be easily read. There it was, swelling and all, just like Eve's, 500123.

Eve had found the photo at the back of a file cabinet belonging to Charles César. For a long time she had avoided it. Too painful. Too deeply painful, a loose thread to a whole tapestry of anguish that Eve in the security of her position could not or perhaps did not need to unravel. But then one day, after a long bout of reading, she found herself taking it out.

In the sweet, quiet light of a summer afternoon, she followed a dust-filled beam to the only visible female face, and it was then that she noticed that the woman in the photo looked exactly like her. Blond, straight hair with bangs, open Germanic features with a thin nose and large, almond eyes, a birdlike upper body and fleshy rounded hips, even the curve of her stomach and V of her crotch were identical.

"She looks exactly like me," she told Charles César when he came home that night. "I'm of German extraction."

"Please," he said, "give me that." And he took the photo and put it in the trash.

"Why do you have that?" she asked, and he replied, off-center, a little strung out, "I don't know. I bought it in Europe a long time ago. It was a mistake. Leave it alone."

But she couldn't leave it alone. She retrieved the photo from the dustbin and hid it, taking it out in secret and staring at it, fascinated. The woman did look exactly like her. And now Eve, an evil little look of defiance on her face, extended her tattooed arm to the woman in the photo and said, "Immortality for you, Eva. You're coming with me into the twenty-first century."

"What?" asked Charles César, coming into the room. "Who are you talking to?"

She turned the photo upside down on the bed. He sat down next to her and stared sexily into her eyes.

" 'Allo. 'Appy birthday," he said.

" 'Allo," she imitated his French accent and smiled.

She was keeping her arms at her sides limp on the bed. He went to pick them up and place them around his neck when he saw the swelling and asked, "What is this?"

She didn't answer. He examined the swelling more closely, then, knowing exactly what it was, he asked again, "What is this?"

"It's her I.D. number." She reached for the photo and showed it to him. "Hers. I call her Eva."

Charles César was stunned. He looked like someone had hit him with a hammer.

"What?" he got out finally.

"The tattoo." She pointed at the woman's arm. "I want to remember her. I want to keep her alive. I'm wearing the tattoo like an MIA bracelet."

Charles César got up and began pacing the room. Eve couldn't tell what was going on with him.

"Why have you done this?" He asked this reasonably but there was a deadness in his eyes. She didn't trust it.

"Well, in a very few years," she began nervously, "the people who lived through the Third Reich will all be dead. And when the people who experienced an event are no longer walking the planet, it's as if that event never existed at all. There'll be books and museums and monuments, but things move so fast now, the only difference between fantasy and history is living people. I'm going to keep Eva alive. She'll go on living, here, with me."

Charles César seized her hand. She lurched forward as he pulled out her arm and examined the tattoo. The numbers were tiny but haunting. Big Dan had done a perfect job.

"Hey!" she said. She had never seen him like this. "Charlie, I know you're angry, but I haven't done this frivolously. Look, people will ask me about the tattoo and I'm going to tell them tales, based on facts from my reading, tales specially chosen for them, so they can identify, so they can learn."

"That fucking reading!" Charles César threw down her arm, got up, and walked away. "You've gone crazy!"

"I haven't gone crazy. On the contrary, I'm trying to get sane. We live in a country suffering from compassion-fatigue. That's what they said last night on the news. So I'm doing my bit, you know?"

"For Christ's sake!" Charles César exploded.

He slammed his fist into the wall.

"What is it? What's wrong?" Eve was shocked.

Charles César was muttering furiously to himself in French. Eve was terrified.

"You can't wear that tattoo," he spat. "It's an affront."

"Please, my darling." She was gesturing with her hands, trying to disperse the rage in the air, "I know it's sacred. It is to me, too. To me, this tattoo is about the fate of women. The tattoo will help me find out about it and at the same time I can—"

"Shit!" Charles César shouted this. "Shit!" He shouted it again.

Eve leapt off the bed and ran to him and grabbed his arms. "What is it? What's going on?" She held his chin and peered into his eyes. They were as black and lifeless as the barrels of a shotgun. "Oh," she said, "I see."

"What?" he asked menacingly. "What?"

He looked like the sternest of members of the Catholic hierarchy.

"You're Jewish, aren't you?" she said.

He detached himself from her and stepped back. He didn't reply.

"Let me wash that and put some antiseptic on." She was referring to his fist, which was now bleeding. She tried to touch him.

"No!" he snapped and hurtled from the room.

Eve sank down on the bed, exhausted. Getting the tattoo was a radical act, she knew that. And it was meant to be a catalyst or a spark, and it was bound to ignite some explosions. Well, already it was doing its job. Already it was exploding his secrets.

So, Charlie is Jewish, she thought. That explained some mysteries: the item she found in his closet, his reaction to the photo of Eva, his hatred of her Nazi readings. She could never read her books around him. She had to stack her histories and witness accounts in a corner and hide them with a cloth so he couldn't see them. And then there was that earthiness about him, a hotness that up until now she had ascribed to Catholicism. She had thought, perhaps, he had Italian or Irish blood, some genetic drop that made the difference. But no, she thought, he's Jewish.

Though Eve trusted herself in hindsight, really she was floored. She and Charlie often had discussions about religion. It was something they had in common. They had both been very religious as children. She was a baptized, confirmed Episcopalian. He, she thought, was a baptized, confirmed Catholic. Hadn't he said so? She racked her brain to remember. In adulthood, they had both ceased attending church except at Christmas and Easter, when they went together and discussed it afterwards.

He had taken the tattoo like a bombshell and now she understood why. But it wasn't meant to be an affront. It was the emblem of a different perspective, the perspective of women, all kinds of women. She looked down at the tattoo, Eva's perspective. And out of that, there was surely something new to be learned. Hitler used to say, "Germany is my bride." He thought of Germany as a woman. And right there, right in that statement was a clue. And when she told Charlie what she'd found out about the Racial Hygiene laws and the Euthanasia Program and how she was trying to put it all together, she was certain he would understand.

But his anger, she thought, as she picked up the photo and balanced it on her lap, his explosive anger was something she hadn't reckoned on. Was that just because she'd found out he was Jewish?

"Jewish, Eva," she said to her look-alike in the photo. "My boyfriend is Jewish. Are you?"

III

It was six-thirty when Eve left the house. Charles César was nowhere to be found. Perhaps he would show up at the party later, cooled off, perhaps not. It would take some time for him to adjust.

She turned the corner and a young man gave her an appreciative glance. She smiled at him. His enjoyment of her was like a round of applause for the care she had taken getting dressed. But then, lately, she was a magnet for men in their twenties.

"You're in your Phaedra period, dear," her Uncle Jim had explained. She laughed.

As she turned off 4th and proceeded up Bank Street, she caught sight of Charles César. He was leaning up against a tree in front of Cilla's brownstone and the atmosphere around him was dark and brooding. She was afraid. As she walked toward him, she took a deep breath to calm herself.

"I'm sorry," she said meekly.

He looked her over, finally focusing on the wrist of her tattooed arm where she wore the bracelet of tiny diamonds he'd given her that morning.

"That's a lovely juxtaposition," he said sardonically.

"The bracelet is lovely," she replied.

"You can't do this, Eve," he warned. "You can't wear that in public. I told you to leave it alone. I told you."

"Leave what alone?" she asked.

He didn't reply.

"It's a testament," she said with defiance. "That's what it is to me—a living testament to Eva. And I will wear it in public because I go out in public and it's part of me now!"

She backed away from him across the pavement. She braced herself against the wrought-iron fence in front of Cilla's brownstone and cradled her tattooed arm.

"You have to clean your house," she warned.

She was referring to Charles César's family. He never spoke of his parents. He never referred to his childhood with them, and when she questioned him about them, he maneuvered away, closing the subject. She felt, from the depth of his secrecy, that perhaps they might have abused him. And now she knew they were Jewish.

"Thank you, pop psychology," he replied.

"Why didn't you tell me?" She asked this gently, soothingly. "I don't care if you're Jewish."

"I'm not Jewish. I'm a Catholic," he replied.

"But your parents were Jewish?" she prodded.

"I converted to Catholicism when I was a child."

"How old?"

"Sixteen."

"A child?"

"Once a Jew, always a Jew," he said bitterly.

"No," she said, and then thinking about it, "I'm sorry. I see what you mean."

"No," he said. "Once a Jew, always a Jew—it's truth."

"And once a WASP, always a WASP?"

"Without question."

"And your Catholicism?"

"Is in my heart. My Judaism is in my soul."

"Really?" she asked. This upset her for some reason.

"So, I can't go out in public with you wearing that," he said. "I'm not going to Cilla and Marcus's. I can't."

"Charlie," Eve said quietly, "They think you're Christian."

He looked away.

"Even so," he said.

"I'm forty today." She bowed her head. She was embarrassed by this. "I don't have children. I want to give someone life. I'm giving Eva life."

He looked back at her. He was furious, his eyes reddened with anguish.

"Get rid of it," he snapped.

"Why are you hiding?" she snapped back.

There was a long silence then, during which they just stared at each other. Finally, Eve roused herself and turned and began walking toward Cilla's brownstone. She sighed heavily.

"Eve," Charlie called. She stopped and faced him. "You know how Christians are just Christians?" he said. "I wanted to be a Jew like that. I didn't want to be a Jew in quotes."

And turning on his heel, he strode off down Bank Street, pausing once to look back and glower at her before he disappeared around a corner.

IV

"Happy birthday, darling."

Cilla threw open the door with great English heartiness and embraced Eve.

"We have a present for you," said her little daughter, Nora, who was four.

"Oh, goody, Nora," said Eve, laughing at how sweet she was, dragging herself gratefully out of the land of angst.

"Where's Charles César?" asked Cilla as she rushed into the kitchen and returned with a tray of canapés.

"He's working late," Eve lied smoothly. "He might not be able to come at all."

"Christ, this city," said Cilla. "Now that people are off drugs, they don't have any fun at all. They'd rather work than have a conversation or fuck or anything. Bores the pants off me."

"Here's the present."

Nora was standing on her tiptoes handing Eve a box. She watched Eve open it with relish.

"Oh, Nora, a bracelet of cats. It's lovely." Eve grabbed Nora and snuggled her. "Thank you. Thank you."

"Put it on," shouted Nora. She was very excited.

"Okay. Help me," shouted Eve and stuck out both wrists.

"Ohhh," said Nora, suddenly frowning. "Did you hurt yourself?"

18   "No. Not exactly," replied Eve.

Nora looked closely at Eve's left forearm, at the tattoo, and then lit up. "Five," she was pointing at the numbers. "Oh-oh-one-two-three."

"That's right, Nora." Eve smiled. "You're doing very well with your counting."

"Eve," Cilla had materialized above them and was staring down at the tattoo. "Darling, what is that? Your supermarket PIN number, I hope? Your cash machine code number, perhaps?"

Cilla looked at her meaningfully and awaited an explanation. Eve looked up at her. It was the first time she would articulate it in public, and she wanted to get it right.

"No," she began. "It's the identification number of an Auschwitz prisoner called Eva."

"Funny," said Cilla. "That's exactly what it looks like. Oh, the doorbell."

As she fled down the hall to the door, Cilla called behind her, "That's washable, isn't it, dear?"

"No, it isn't," Eve called after her. "It's on there for life."

About half an hour later, all the guests, with the exception of Charles César, had arrived and were strewn about the living room. Besides Cilla and her husband, Marcus, there were three other couples, all very close friends of Eve, people who loved her as much as anyone who has a career and a love life and parents in this modern world can be said to love anyone else. But if there is a test, these were people who, if Eve were dying and they had the most important meeting of their lives, would cut the meeting short to come to her deathbed. All but Cilla, who would cancel the meeting, but then she had left England pre-Thatcher and still believed life was in the living of it.

The news of Eve's tattoo had, by this time, swept the party. It was Nora who had informed everyone. As each couple had arrived, Nora had thrown open the door and announced, "Eve has a tattoo, like in the circus."

This had led each couple to approach Eve and ask, "What's

this about a tattoo?" To which Eve had hastily replied, "I'll tell you later," and all the men had forgotten about it. The women, however, had not. They had believed Nora, checked out the tattoo, and, as soon as Eve had gone upstairs to the bathroom, clustered in the kitchen whispering to Cilla about it.

"Oh, boy. This is some midlife crisis," said Babe, a brilliant woman in her early forties who had refused, ever, to support herself.

"Midlife crisis? She looks about thirty-five. I just pray I look that good at her age," said Marie, who was thirty-five and possessed of a gentle Victorian beauty and manner. Marie, through ill fate, was an A&R person in the music business.

"She's turned forty, darling," said Cilla to Marie, "something you know nothing about, bless your innocence. Turning forty is a dilemma. Should one spring for a handgun or collagen injections? There's no easy answer."

"Whose number is it?" asked Alice. She was, like Eve, a humor writer, but of the gentle sort, in her late thirties and motherly, protective.

"A woman called Eva. That's all she told me," said Cilla.

"Eva?" Babe and Alice said this simultaneously and giggled.

"Uh-oh," said Alice.

"She made that up. I can feel it," said Babe. "It's a bizarre overidentification."

"Eve isn't Jewish, is she?" Marie was a lapsed Catholic except at Christmas.

"No," replied Cilla, who was Church of England. "She's a WASP. Episcopalian, I think."

"Is Eva Jewish?" asked Alice, who was Jewish turned Hindu turned Jewish.

"Gee, I hope so," said Babe. Babe was Jewish but she'd married a Catholic. She hadn't celebrated a Jewish holiday since 1972.

"Babe!" the women said together.

"I'm sorry. I'm sorry," said Babe throwing up her hands, and a pall descended over the kitchen.

"Christ," said Marie sadly, "why'd she do this? What does it mean?"

"I wonder what Charles César thinks of it," mused Cilla. She opened the oven and checked the roast.

"He's Catholic, isn't he?" asked Babe.

"Yes," said Cilla. "And French, of course. I adore the French, but they did kill one of my ancestors at the battle of Agincourt."

"God," said Alice, "it's a wonder anybody in Europe speaks to each other."

"I'll drink to that," replied Cilla and removed the roast from the oven.

Eve came down the stairs, realized all the women were in the kitchen, and fled quickly into the living room where she knew, for the moment, she would be safe. The men were draped over the sofa and mantle like huge water birds with their wings half-spread. Nora was standing nearby at the plastic microwave she had received for Christmas. With a look of resignation, she was cooking a rubber muffin.

"I'd like mine well done," Eve said to Nora.

"We're closed," Nora replied.

Eve laughed. "This early?" she asked.

Nora wiped her brow. "Yes. I've had it."

Eve shook her head. "Oh, not so young, Nora. Impossible."

The men turned as Eve left Nora and came toward them. They had been talking about sports, that strange language of male politesse and camaraderie with its odd numerical idioms and high-energy rhythms.

"They're three and oh," Marcus was shouting, and then when he saw her, he dropped his voice and said, "Happy birthday, darling, sit down here"——quite another voice for the women.

"How old are you?"

Alice's date, Benny Slinky, a young, gay editor for a fashion magazine, came over and perched on the arm of her chair.

"The same age Jack Benny was when he died," Eve said. The other men laughed.

"Who was Jack Benny again?" the young man asked.

"He was a comedian who died suddenly at the age of thirty-six," Eve replied.

"Wasn't he thirty-nine?" asked Marcus, confused.

"No," said Eve and closed the subject.

Babe's husband, Doug, who was an artist and spoke little, grinned sleepily and sexily at Eve across the room. He winked his greeting.

"Hi, Doug," Eve called. "How's the art world? You all look so rich now. I miss those paint-spattered jeans."

Doug nodded and laughed silently.

Marie's husband, Les, who was a record producer and had the depleted air of a man who summered in a soundproof environment, came over to Eve and kissed her on the lips.

"I remember," he began, "standing in front of the Dom on St. Mark's Place when this white-blond vision appeared: skirt up to her crotch, see-through blouse, thigh boots, and that bone-straight hair, and I said to myself—man it's true, the fifties are finally over."

"I remember that," Eve said, "dimly."

Actually she remembered it very well. Les, shirtless, wearing hip-hugger jeans and boots, his black hair scraggling to his waist, defiantly smoking a joint. He was eighteen, skinny with big shoulders, the outline of every little muscle visible through his skin. Yes, she remembered saying to him, I believe the fifties are over, too, but they lurk inside of us and we must never let down our guard. And with that, they became friends. He had no place to live and so she took him home where he shared the bed of BeeBee, a doll-faced English model who was crashing at her place for the duration.

Eve remembered this but she didn't like to. Recently a terrible feeling had come over her that youth was just a betrayal, a scrumptious bait the gods set out to trap you. Once trapped, they wrenched youth away from you overnight leaving you hungry and tired and facing the next forty years of decay as
22 fearful and innocent as the day you were born. Far from being

the neat life cycle that Shakespeare envisioned, with old age returning to infancy, Eve found in the middle a ludicrous rebirth. And mewling and puking, she had gotten the tattoo, which she glanced at now between knowing smiles and which instantly made her feel calm.

"Dinner," called Cilla, and the women flooded out of the kitchen carrying dishes.

Eve and the men rose and walked over to the table.

"Where do you want us?" Eve asked.

And Cilla arranged them. Eve was sitting between Marcus and Les across from Babe. Cilla and the other women set the food dishes on the table and sat down. Nora had eaten but she settled herself at a little table near the big table and pretended to chew the rubber muffin. Cilla removed the setting for Charles César and urged everybody to take more room.

"Where's Charlie?" Marcus asked as everyone scooted over.

"Editing," mumbled Eve.

"Isn't it dreadful, on her birthday," pronounced Cilla and began to pass the food.

The women glanced at each other. They knew Charles César wasn't editing. They could tell by the look on Eve's face.

"He'll come later, won't he?" asked Marie kindly.

"I don't know," answered Eve. "He may. He's very busy now. The Afghan film's almost done and he's a bit driven what with the Russian pullout."

"Yes," said Cilla, "it should be a new can of worms there with the Russians gone."

"Well, same can, different worms," said Eve and reached across the table for the vegetables.

"God, that bracelet's beautiful," gasped Alice, fixing on the tiny diamonds encircling Eve's tattoo. "Did Charlie give you that?"

"Yes. Isn't it something?"

Eve turned her wrist around like a hand model, mesmerizing the women with the diamonds, confounding them with the tattoo.

23

"Well," said Alice, "he doesn't have to show if he gave you diamonds, for God's sake. I bet you uttered the phrase I have always longed to say: 'You shouldn't have.' Anyone at this table ever have cause to say 'You shouldn't have'?"

"No."

"Nope."

"No."

The men and women shook their heads.

"See," said Alice, "you're a lucky girl, Eve."

Eve laughed. "I know it," she said.

"What's that?"

Doug, to everyone's amazement, had clasped Eve's wrist and was pointing at the tattoo. Usually he stayed away from the sticky situations, leaving them to the capable hands of Babe. Maybe he just didn't sense it, or the artist in him was intrigued by the inking. At any rate, the table went silent and waited.

Eve turned to him and muttered, "Et tu, Brute?"

Everyone giggled nervously.

"Well . . ."

Eve sighed deeply. She was afraid. It was her first—what would she call it—performance, no, enlightenment, specially chosen for this audience. She prayed it would go well.

"It's a tattoo, a replica of the tattoo given to a Jewish prisoner at Auschwitz called Eva Klein. I'm wearing it like an MIA bracelet."

Doug nodded. "Where'd you have it done?" he asked.

The women contacted each other. Already the men had changed the subject.

"Big Dan's Tattoo Parlor in upstate New York. Amazing place. A monument to male violence. Big Dan has made a fetish out of insensitivity. Biker stuff. Nazi stuff. Vietnam stuff. But I doubted him. I had to ask myself, has he really waded in blood?"

"Pass the brussels sprouts, please," said Cilla.

"A lot of rock bands have tattoos now," offered Les. "It's really in."

24   There was a pause during which the women eyed each

other. Who would ask Eve? Should it be done kindly, forcefully, analytically? Babe abdicated. She didn't trust herself. Cilla, too. She wasn't an American. It fell to Alice and Marie, who glanced at each other, with Alice bowing to Marie's lead. Benny Slinky, who thrived on tension and so hardly noticed it, said, between gulps of food, "You know, I couldn't care less about the Nazis. It's ancient history. I couldn't give a fuck."

"The Nazis were masters of S&M, Benny. That interests you," said Babe. She couldn't help herself.

"That's true," Benny said, nodding thoughtfully.

"It's all right," said Eve. "You're twenty-six years old. Your parents weren't in World War Two. You were educated in the seventies, which is an oxymoron. Why should you care?"

"I saw *Holocaust,* the miniseries," offered Benny hopefully.

"I lost quite a few relatives in the war," sniffed Marcus, "both wars."

Marie saw a space and leapt into it.

"Who was Eva Klein?" she asked.

She turned to Benny and put her finger on her lips. The men and women at the table turned to Eve.

"Eva Klein," repeated Eve looking around the table but, really, looking back into herself. "Eva Klein was a U-boat. That's what the Jews hiding out in Berlin from 'forty-two to 'forty-four called themselves. U-boats, like the Nazi submarines. Because unless they were walled up in an attic or something, they had to leave the apartments in which they were hidden during the day, and prowl the streets until nightfall. Anyone in the house all day in wartime Germany was instantly suspect.

"Eva was a yuppie. She was in her thirties and married to a guy her own age who was a successful gems dealer. They had a child, a girl, who was a year old at the time they were called for deportation by the Gestapo and went into hiding."

Cilla glanced over at Nora and smiled protectively.

"Hans, Eva's husband, had made a lot of money before the war, dealing diamonds, and his expertise continued to be salable to the wartime black market. So they were luckier than most

Jews in hiding because Hans was always able to make some money."

They hid separately, Eve went on. Eva and the baby stayed in a rooming house in a residential part of the city. Hans shared an apartment with the family of a Gentile accountant who had been in his employ. Hans and Eva saw each other sporadically. Hans just appeared once or twice a month bearing food. The rest of the time, Eva walked in the city's parks.

Eva and Hans had been in hiding for about a year. The baby was now two. So far things had gone pretty well. Eva looked Aryan. She was blond and blue-eyed and snub-nosed, a paradigm of racial eugenics, so there was no trouble there. She had learned to enter any place labeled "No Jews Allowed" without a drop of guilt or terror. She had even mastered her facial expressions. The look on her face was always happy, carefree and happy, for it was said that one could tell the Jews hiding out by the sad, hunted looks on their faces. But not Eva. She had learned to laugh at everything.

It was the winter of '43 and life was becoming more difficult. Daylight bombing had begun, which meant it was more dangerous in the parks. There was often chaos in the streets and food was getting scarce. The baby was more mobile now and less controllable. She didn't sleep as easily as she had and Eva worried constantly about her tan. When the baby was one, Eva had dressed her in wide-brimmed bonnets. But now that she was two, she refused to wear them. Since Eva was obliged to take her out from 8 a.m. to 5 p.m., every day, rain or shine, traipsing from one park to another, the baby was developing a strong skier's tan. It was a dead giveaway. And Eva was becoming exhausted.

The baby did not yet talk, probably because Eva was always shushing her, rewarding her for silence. So it came as a great shock to Eva, one late afternoon, when, in a park near the Wilhelmstrasse, the baby spoke her first words.

It had been a long day. There had been a bombing raid with all its accompanying horror. They had been forced to enter an air-raid shelter, which meant confronting people, possibly "catchers"—those Jews hired by the Gestapo to hunt down Jews—and all that angst. Then they had returned to the parks and it had rained, so they had gone to the newsreels. But the baby started screaming there, and they had had to leave. By four o'clock they were both pretty wrung out. The baby was running frantically in the grass, flinging bits of shrapnel at Eva, putting other bits in her mouth, shrieking. Eva was reprimanding her, telling her to shush, when all of a sudden the baby rushed up to her, grabbed her by the arms, and, with a look of depthless fury shouted, "I want to go home."

Eva wept as she tried to explain. "We can't go home yet, darling. I wish we could, too. But we can't. We just can't." The baby roared and, for the first time, Eva just let her. She quickly wiped away her own tears, however, and began laughing so that when a policeman passed and looked at them curiously, she was able to giggle, rolling her eyes in embarrassment, like a young mother who's momentarily lost control.

But Eva had lost control. She felt terror instead of joy that her baby had begun to talk, and that all but unhinged her. In the evening, when Hans showed up and, once again, was unable to make love to her, she realized that she could not go on. She made Hans take the baby, and the next day she was spotted by a catcher and was arrested. Eva died at Auschwitz while on an exterior work detail. Hans and the baby survived the war.

Eve lowered her eyes to indicate that her tale had ended. "Oh, God," said Cilla immediately. "Come here, Nora."

The child ran over and Cilla hugged her to her breast. Nora struggled and pushed her mother away.

"No. Grownup now," Nora said.

The company stared at Nora for a moment and then went back to eating in silence. Finally Marie said, "I've got to call my babysitter. Excuse me."

She rose and left the room.

"Me, too," said Alice and followed her out.

Benny turned to Eve and said soberly,

"What was the story with the Nazis, anyway?"

"Good luck, Eve," said Babe.

"It's not a simple topic, Benny, but you can start with this: a psychotic obsession with glory, a murderous mania for purity, and a visceral hatred of women. In the end, the variety of humanity was intolerable to the Nazis. They murdered fifteen million people in the camps alone, not to mention those they did away with in prisons, cities, and villages throughout the occupied territories.

"They murdered Jews, Poles, Czechs, French, Russians, Hungarians, Greeks, Yugoslavs, British, Americans, gypsies, homosexuals, criminals, the homeless, the retarded, the disabled, Communists, Socialists, intellectuals, artists, actors, magazine editors, and on and on, oh, and Jehovah's Witnesses. Though why they went for Jehovah's Witnesses is a mystery to me right now."

Cilla, Marcus, and Babe contacted each other uncomfortably across the table.

"Jehovah's Witnesses," said Benny excitedly. "Yeah, that's right. You know, if it were happening today, Michael Jackson would be gassed."

"I never thought of that, Benny," said Babe. "Thanks."

V

When Eve got back to the loft, Charles César was sleeping. She flopped herself down in the living area and gazed out the windows at the Empire State Building shimmering in pastel light. She was forty, forty. She rolled this over in her mind and still couldn't believe it. The previous year, Israel had turned forty and had seemed to go mad. She had written about it in her column. If I were Israel and I were turning forty, I'd fuck every Arab in sight too, she had written then, correctly foreseeing that a madness combined with a great sexual urge would overtake her about this time. What she hadn't foreseen was the compulsive drive toward some buoy in a sea of disposable knowledge, and, of course, that sense of betrayal.

She glanced down at her forearm. The swelling was all but gone now. The tattoo was perfect and terrible. She was pleased with its effect on the dinner party. Eva Klein had been the right choice. Even Benny Slinky had been visibly moved, not a pretty sight but a rare one.

Everyone had identified. For a few minutes the tattoo had jolted them from the lethe of middle-class life and they suddenly looked not sophisticated or cynical, not fed up or bored, not played-out or wired, just human, exposed, their expressions softened with an empathy they would never have acknowledged that they could feel.

"Okay," Benny Slinky had said sadly, "okay. I'll go see *Night and Fog* the next time it plays at an art house."

And he meant it.

Eve ran her finger over the tattoo. It still hurt a little. She took up her purse, removed the bacitracin ointment from it, and unscrewed the top. As she smoothed the salve across the inky numbers, she thought about Eva. Who was Eva? Why was she arrested? Was she married? Did she have children?

Eve had created the tale of Eva Klein from facts she read in a history of five hundred Jews who remained hidden in Berlin up until the end of the war. She had chosen Eva Klein partly because she was Jewish—that was for Babe and Alice—and partly because she was a parent dealing with a baby under hellish circumstances. With that the others at the table could identify. As for Benny, well, she just took a chance and it had seemed to work. He had once told her he identified with every mother on earth except Mother Theresa, whom he found too good to be true.

It was Eve's observation that, in the forty-five years since the war, Americans had simplified the hideous phenomenon that was the Third Reich, tying it up into a neat package labeled: MAD HITLER—KILLED JEWS. Eve had done that herself. For years she read histories and witness accounts, and, though she found them profoundly disturbing, she always had an out. A little WASP voice in her brain would shield her. I would have been okay, it echoed. I'm not Jewish. I would have been safe.

And then one day, not long after she came across the photo of Eva, she was reading a history of Nazism that had been favorably reviewed in the newspaper and she stumbled upon a snippet of information about something called the Euthanasia Program in Nazi Germany. It was just a passing reference but it said that the first mass gassing of innocent human beings had taken place on January 4, 1940, at an asylum in Brandenburg, near Berlin. Those gassed were non-Jewish German mental patients. What? Eve's brain said. What? I thought they invented it at Auschwitz. I thought they developed it to kill Jews. She reread the passage again to make sure she had read it right. She had. The Nazis had invented mass gassing to kill non-Jewish Germans. Their first mass gassing murdered only Aryan Germans.

That one little fact opened doors in Eve's mind that led her to getting the tattoo. Doors of identification, doors of terror, doors that led to rooms of questions she had never thought to ask, from perspectives she had never considered. She set about reading whatever she could find, and there wasn't much, on the Euthanasia Program, and that led her to the Racial Hygiene laws, and what she read changed the little WASP echo in her brain. It could have been you, it now said. It would have been you.

Eve got up, turned off the lights, and stood for a moment taking in the beauty of a pink-and-blue Empire State Building. Some things modern man had created were truly stunning, really haunting, but just some, she thought.

She went off down the hall to the bedroom, undressed, performed her ablutions, and after greeting the photo of Eva, which she had hidden under the bed, climbed in next to Charles César. She did a flip of the TV channels and, at one loud advertisement, Charlie lifted his tousled head and saw she was back. With a free hand, she muted the TV sound.

"Everyone sent their love," Eve said. "Where did you go?"

"To a bar. I got drunk."

"How retro of you. Soon you'll be having sex."

"I hope so."

He reached over and caressed her nipple. He was the only man Eve had ever known who could fuck when he was furious.

"Wait." She whispered, grabbing his hand.

"All right," he sighed.

"I still love you even though you're Jewish," she said.

He was silent.

"Have you lost your sense of humor now?" she asked.

"It's possible," he replied.

"Can I ask you something?"

31

He nodded.

"If you spent the first sixteen years of your life Jewish, do you really believe in the Christian doctrine? Christ—the resurrection, the afterlife, you know?"

He looked over at her. She really wanted to know the answer.

"I don't know," he said quietly. "I try to. I want to."

"Oh," she said. "Because we've talked so much, we—"

"I've always said this. You've asked me this before."

"Well, I know, but—So where do you go after death?"

"I don't know," he said. "Perhaps nowhere."

"Not to heaven or hell? Not to God?" Her voice rose when she asked this. She didn't mean it to.

"I don't know," he answered.

"I see myself up there with the Father, Son, and Holy Ghost. We're having lofty conversation. They're very handsome. When I was little, it was more abstract. So, what is it? Just in the ground, rotting?"

In spite of herself, she felt disgusted by this.

"I don't know," he said again.

"Oh," she replied. "Oh."

She was silent for a time. Then she said, "I need to find out about the women. Christian women in Nazi Germany. How did they accept Nazism, facism? I don't understand it. I was taught the message of Christianity is love, you know? Loving thy neighbor, kindness, mercy, generosity—what today we call codependence—how could they deny that? How could they be Christian and do what they did? How did their hearts get so hardened? I am implicated by association. That's another reason I got the tattoo."

"You are so naïve," Charlie said, taking her hand.

"Maybe," she said. "We'll see."

"Eve," he asked, stroking her fingers, "how do you really feel about my being Jewish?"

Eve looked away.

"You said you converted."

"I did."

"Is there something else you want to tell me?"

"No."

"What then? Do you want to know if I've slept with other Jews?"

"Have you?"

"No."

"Never?" He couldn't believe this.

"No. Not by design. It just never happened."

"Even in the sixties?"

"I slept with one man from 1966 through 1972 and he was a WASP. They were all WASPS. I don't care, Charlie. I don't care if you were Golda Meir as a child."

"It's not real to you, yet."

"What are you saying to me?" she asked.

"Nothing," he replied. "Look at me."

She stared at him. He smiled and his eyes sparkled. The little crucifix he wore around his neck gleamed in the light.

"So," he said softly, "I'm your first."

He gathered her wrists in one hand and pinned them over her head. Then, with mock cruelty, he began sucking her nipple. In mock restraint she twisted her wrists and his hand pressed the tattoo.

"Ow!" she cried, and wrenched her wrists out of his grip.

Surprised, he looked up, saw the tattoo, and lost his erection.

"Ah," he muttered.

She gazed nervously into his eyes.

He moved off her and lay by her side.

"No," he whispered. "I can't make love to you with that on there, with what it makes me see."

"Charlie, she was a woman just like me, not a skinny old corpse, not a death's head."

"Hatred and sadism, every association I have. I can't tell you."

Eve took his hand. "Look, she made love and laughed before the Nazis got her. She wasn't what they made her into in the   33 end. I think it's perverse to think that she was, or any of them were. Don't you?"

"I don't know."

"What responsibility do you and I have to a mound of skeletons in a mass grave murdered before we were conceived? None. But to the people those skeletons once were? Infinite."

Charles César did not reply. He turned his body toward the wall.

"Good night," he murmured.

"Good night, Charlie," she replied.

Eve stared mindlessly at the TV for quite some time before she did a flip. When she did, she clicked right to the twenty-four-hour news station and turned up the sound. A young German woman was speaking. Hungary had opened its borders and made it possible for East Germans to escape to the West. The young woman had fled. She was thrilled and beaming with light.

All week, Eastern Europe had been in turmoil. The Communist government in Poland had fallen and Lech Walesa had been elected president. Now Hungary was doing this odd thing with its borders.

They had gotten fed up, Eve thought. After forty years, they could no longer stand the grimness, grayness, and lack of humor that seemed to be the Communist world. Who could blame them? Actually, for years she had found it hard to believe that Eastern Europe really was that grim. It seemed impossible. Western propaganda. Who could live like that? But it turned out that it really was that grim and here were these Germans pouring out of Communist Germany, cloaked in the mantle of freedom, and making up for forty years of not smiling.

But somehow, Eve felt sorry for the woman on TV. Because she was so innocent and trusting. Because she had no idea of the complexities ahead of her. Pretty soon, Eve thought, she'll be wondering who gave her chlamydia, how to get cash for her weekend drugs, and if her name's on the A-list for parties. She'll feel the hurt as much as she felt the restriction, only she won't know how to resist.

"We have no enemy here, sweetheart, only the self," Eve said to her. "You'll find out."

Charles César stirred. Eve muted the sound.

For a long time she stared down at him, examining his features, taking in this new person with whom she was sharing her bed. He looked, she always thought, like a sexy Vatican cardinal. Partly this was because of the skirted French jackets he wore all the time. He had them made in France and they were beautifully cut. When he left a room, the skirt of his jacket flapped behind him. Like priests in their cassocks at her school, flapping around corners. But it was also because of his nose, his aquiline and, she had always thought, long, Roman nose. A sexy Vatican cardinal, she had always thought. And the wise expression in his eyes. But, like much of the matrix of love, it was just an illusion.

What was it the girls used to say at lunch? Jews make the best husbands. Jews are better in bed. Well, she had always denied these things, holding up Charlie as an example. And the girls would say, Oh, well, he's foreign. It doesn't count.

She burrowed down next to him. Mingus, their Siamese cat, bounded onto the bed and inserted his warm body between them. It wasn't until she was almost asleep that it occurred to her: if Charlie's parents were Jewish and they were French, they would have been French Jews in Nazi-occupied France.

VI

Eve was a political satirist by profession. She wrote a monthly column for a men's magazine, and her satirical voice was so blunt and cruel that, though it made her laugh, it surprised her. The man she lived with before Charles César had been embarrassed by her pieces even though she commanded a great deal of respect, and so she learned to hide her work when her man came home and behave instead like a hostess from the 1950s.

This was fine with Eve. She loved being a geisha. She loved doing housework, cooking dinners, going to exercise class, shopping, and she was very pretty. So, it worked. But it came as quite a shock whenever she was introduced to someone who knew her only from her writing.

"They always expect a lady in a hat carrying a knife," she would tell Babe. "Somewhere, that's me."

To Charles César's credit, he found this dual personality of Eve's somewhat bizarre. He was a fan of Eve's writing and had expected her to be satirical and intellectual as a European counterpart might be. Instead, he told his French male friends, he had moved in with Donna Reed, a cheerful, perfect TV housewife who agreed with most things he said and was, forever, gentling him out of bad humors. In secret, she had this steel-trap mind that turned out pieces like "How to Tell if Your Girlfriend Is Dying During Rough Sex," or, "Dennis Thatcher's How to Live with a Famous Person for Fifteen Minutes," and who described herself as a "female supremacist." But she never showed it. In the two years they had lived together, he had encouraged her to merge the two personalities but she found it difficult. So when she got the tattoo, it was a personal breakthrough for Eve as well as a victory for Charles César. It was just bad luck that it struck at his very heart and soul.

Several weeks had passed since the dinner party, and Eve was glued to the TV. The Eastern Europeans were breaking out. First the Poles, now the Hungarians, had revised their constitutions to allow multiparty systems. Gorbachev was visiting East Germany for its fortieth anniversary, and demonstrations were erupting in Leipzig.

Fortieth birthday, thought Eve, there it is again, a dangerous, eruptive time. A fight for a new life or, as in the case of Israel, a struggle against it. It all depended on your personality and the cards God dealt you. In the case of Eastern Europeans it was as if after forty years of life, they had just found love and nothing, nothing was going to stop them from consummating it.

Eve was in the bedroom. She was just removing her typewriter from the closet where she kept it hidden, when Charles César came in. She felt startled and exposed. She put the typewriter back, closed the closet door, and started talking.

"Can you believe these Communists are denying Communism? It's so demeaning. Can they mean it? I don't trust these newsmen. They don't speak foreign languages and they tell us things they make up.

"Take Tianamen Square. Within two days they were telling us it was revolution. It wasn't revolution. The students just wanted to talk to the governing body of the university. By the time the TV newsmen had been there two weeks, it was revolution."

"Are you saying it was our fault?"

"I'm saying the TV newsmen made the Chinese government lose global face. And when the Chinese lose face, watch out. The worst is possible."

"This is a radical viewpoint."

Charles César looked at Eve curiously. Eve had lived in China when she was small. Her father had been a diplomat. She had an understanding of the Chinese people that was accurate and uncanny. That first day of Tianamen Square, Charlie had come home and the twenty-four-hour news station was broadcasting live coverage of Chinese students playing guitars and sitting-in. It was rather peaceful, he thought. But Eve was crying.

"This is going to end terribly," she told him through her tears. "Tanks, executions."

He hadn't believed her. When her prediction came true, he asked her how she had known but she refused to speak about it. This was the first he had heard of it since then.

"It is not a radical viewpoint," she went on. "It is understanding another culture. Losing face is one of the worst things that could happen to a Chinese. There is no recouping. The Chinese value their children above all else. Killing them with tanks and executions is a tragedy inexplicable by any other reasoning."

"What are you writing about this month?"

Charles César took the opportunity to get more information. Eve realized he had caught her spouting off, and she blushed.

"Oh, I don't know. Want some breakfast, darling?"

Eve reached up to caress his cheek, but he saw the tattoo and moved away. It was now some time since they'd had sex. The strain was beginning to show.

"I told you to get rid of that!" he said.

Eve turned the sound on the TV up.

"Eve . . . Eve!"

He was angry now.

"Charlie, were your parents victims of the holocaust? Is that why you can't look at the tattoo? Is that why it turns you off so? Were they in the camps?"

"Get rid of it!" he said.

"Please let me help you. Please let me——"

"Get rid of it!" he shouted.

38   And she just sat back on the bed and stared at him. He was

like a different person. He was becoming a different person.

After a time she said, "Look at these Eastern Europeans on TV, hundreds of thousands of them risking their lives. It's humbling. Look at the determination in their faces, the energy. I wish we felt that here, don't you? I can't even imagine what might get us to feel like that again. This makes me feel bad about America, about the hopelessness we've been feeling."

Charles César stared at the TV. Ever since Eve had gotten the tattoo, she talked of politics. And while that turned him on, he was so despairing about the tattoo, he couldn't touch her. After all, he left France because the memory of Nazism dogged his life and deprived him of joy. It was his curse. And, in the end, he had not escaped it. It turned up here, in a loft in New York City, in, of all souring places, his bed.

"You don't know what hopelessness is," he said. "I've got to go. I'll be back late."

And he stalked out of the room.

Eve went back to the TV. The number of East Germans streaming to the West had reached one hundred thousand. Visuals of young people driving hellbent toward a new life in their funny, Communist-made autos flashed before her. Visuals of weeping mothers left behind in cramped Eastern Bloc apartments followed. Eve made notes for a column.

Families torn asunder by external forces was the big story in the outside world, she noted, from South Africa to Germany. In America, the story of the family was one of internecine strife. So Americans in their inventive, futuristic way had come up with something new to take the family's place: the self-help group, the recovery program. Free family for everybody and no strings attached.

And yet, Eve thought, when she went to Smokers Anonymous, she often left there feeling contempt for those who still smoked. She felt distaste for their impurity and weakness. She hated their smokers' characteristics. And because they sparked her craving, she wanted them away. Just like the Nazis, she thought. Maybe that's it—maybe Man is always trying to get

clean. His obsession with his own dirtiness is ultimately patho-
logical and murderous. Original sin. Is that the link we have
with them?

It interested Eve that Hitler was a rabid antismoker. He was
a nondrinker and a vegetarian. Well, she thought, that certainly
belies the red-meat-equals-aggression myth.

Mingus, the cat, jumped onto her lap and she stroked him
and thought about Eva. Eve had been reading a book about the
role of women in Nazi Germany. The book said that women had
overwhelmingly supported Hitler right from the beginning, actually keeping the party alive through fund-raising when Hitler
was imprisoned in 1928.

Extraordinary, Eve thought. Hitler couldn't have made it
without the women. And Shirer had said in his memoirs that at
the Nuremburg rallies, the women went into a trance when
Hitler spoke. She'd seen film of it. The women's faces were
upturned and blissful, ecstasy lit up their eyes. They screamed
for him and waved their flags. Their reaction was exactly like
that of girls she'd seen mobbing the Beatles in the 1960s. The
women adored Hitler. They were in love with him. That was
clear. But Eve couldn't see why. When she saw footage of him
in documentaries, he looked like a martinet, angry and mean,
shrieking at the top of his lungs. Well, she thought, maybe you
had to be there.

Of course, the atmosphere at the rallies had a lot to do with
it. Albert Speer was the genius responsible for that. The graphic
design, the lighting, the orchestration, all had already gone
down in history. A musician had told her that Speer was the first
person ever to modulate voice timbre through a microphone.
He had done this to make Hitler's voice more pleasing to the
crowd. Well, it didn't come through in documentaries, Eve
thought, if it was true.

The book said that Hitler had promised a husband for every
woman and no more having to work. If you put it that way,
no wonder the women supported him. Eve glanced at the tattoo. I wonder if Eva did.

VII

Eve walked into the nondescript room and sat down on one of a circle of chairs. Three or four people were already seated and several others were filtering through the door. Everyone looked tense and slightly angry. Their movements were jerky and their manners abrupt. It was a roomful of people withdrawing from nicotine, a Smokers Anonymous meeting, and the atmosphere was strange and erratic.

For about four months prior to getting the tattoo, Eve had attended this meeting twice or sometimes even three times a week. She was a regular and people recognized her and accorded her a kind of senior status. Except for one fellow who had been going to meetings for two years and never could seem to get over his cravings, Eve was the most reliable person in the room. Others came and went, but Eve and Bob were always there Tuesdays and Fridays, and their dedication was an inspiration to several other people who only stayed off cigarettes because of them.

Among these other people were Cathy and Barbara, seated at the end of the circle opposite Eve, and to whom she now nodded, and Tim, who was just entering the door snarling.

"Goddamn fucking cabdriver! I'd like to rip his fucking throat out! Why doesn't he go back to fucking Pakistan where he belongs if he can't learn goddamn English!"

Tim dropped into a chair and nodded hostilely at those assembled.

"Goddamn cabdrivers," he continued to mutter under his breath.

The group leader, a gay woman in her early forties, entered carrying a sheaf of papers, and settled herself in the center chair of the circle. She glanced up at the clock.

"Okay," she said. "I think we should start. I'm Gay and I'm a nicotine addict."

Cathy and Barbara looked at each other.

"I mean, that's my name—Gay." The leader laughed suavely.

Cathy and Barbara giggled. Eve, Bob, and Tim laughed politely.

"We'll recite the prayer at the end. Let's start by going in a circle."

The leader inclined her head toward Eve, giving her a nod of recognition as she did so. The gay woman didn't always lead this group, but she knew that Eve and Bob were linchpins and she behaved with proper deference. Eve began, "Hi, I'm Eve and I'm sorry to have to tell you this so suddenly, but—I won't be coming for a while."

There were audible gasps around the room. Tim's face was nearly purple. Eve went on.

"I no longer feel a craving for cigarettes and I don't want to talk about them. Last week I got this tattoo and everything changed."

She held up her forearm for all to see. They all leaned forward in their chairs, looked at it, and sat back.

"Of course you know you're never cured," said Bob with concern. "Once a nicotine addict, always a nicotine addict. You're in denial, Eve."

"What are you talking about? What the hell's going on? I depended on you!" Tim shouted this in a tortured tone of voice.

"Cool it, mister," said Gay icily.

"I haven't smoked in a month 'cause of you, Eve," whined

Cathy. "And of course, because of Bob. But, forgive me, Bob, I think the female role model is very influential in my case because of my mother's food addiction taking up so much of her time."

"What's this tattoo, Eve," asked Barbara aggressively. "Is it like a staple in the ear? Can I get one? Does it really stop withdrawal?"

"No, it's not like that," Eve said. "It's the I.D. number of an Auschwitz prisoner from World War Two."

She held up her forearm again and everyone peered at it.

"Oh, it's just a psychological thing," said Barbara, deflated.

"Can't you have that and come to meetings?" pleaded Cathy.

"What—you mean like the Jews—what? I don't understand you," snapped Tim.

Gay drew herself up and addressed them all. "You don't attack the person who's sharing. You don't comment. You sit quietly and provide them with a safe space."

She turned to Tim. "You hear me, buddy?"

"Fuck you," Tim said.

"What'd you say?" Gay stood up and clenched her fists.

"Fuck you. I said, 'Fuck you.' "

Tim stood up and stuck out his chin. Eve stood up and separated the pugilists.

"Sit down. Sit down," Eve cooed softly. "I want to tell you about this woman. I want to tell you about my tattoo."

Gay and Tim glared at each other and dropped silently into their seats. Eve smiled sweetly at them and then began her tale.

"Her name was Eva Hofler. She was thirty-six. And on this day I'm going to tell you about in 1934, she had just discovered she was pregnant. She was very relieved. She had had two miscarriages the previous year and her neighbors were beginning to talk. She prayed this one would hold. The doctor had told her to take it very easy and had filed the papers to inform the state of her good fortune. She considered this pregnancy a birthday present, and as she hurried to the meeting of her church group, she looked forward to the party they would hold for her. It was a tradition. The executive committee always celebrated each other's birthdays."

Hitler had come to power the previous year, Eve went on, and as Eva walked into the parish house, she stopped and looked up with some pride at the Nazi flags that now festooned it. Eva had high hopes of the Nazis. She hoped they would do away with the pornography and decadence that had made Berlin so notorious in the past decade. They were for motherhood and home, which was a relief after the women's emancipation movement of the Weimar period—which made her feel, well, useless, and also nervous about her desire to be a housewife. In fact, if she thought about it, she really liked a lot of things about them.

A few weeks earlier, Eva had attended her first Nazi rally. She'd found it utterly transforming. There were thousands of people there, thousands, all carrying candles, and the swastikas and banners stood above her bathed in these soft lights that swooped about the throng like angels. She waited, for what seemed like hours, while the excitement built, and then suddenly Hitler appeared. And when he spoke, he was so sure and so inspired, and so filled with urgency, it made her heart soar. He was the most exciting person she had ever seen. His rally was the most exciting thing that had ever happened to her. And what he wanted for her—for she felt he was speaking to her personally—was what God wanted for her and for every woman. Only when he spoke to her, it was different from the priests in church. Hitler made her feel as if she would be part of God, too, as if by being the wife and mother that she was, she already had ascended to God. She felt it. She felt it with all her heart. She felt power.

Hitler said he would clean up Germany and Eva was surely for that. The beggars, the crime, the filth, the pornography, had depressed and offended her so. He would get rid of that. He was against decadent art and movies and she was, too. She agreed with his attitudes on race. He had made those sterilization laws to limit families of idiots and insane people, which made sense. Her husband had a job again and was in a good mood. It was a miracle. Hitler had performed a miracle. Maybe he was sent by God. Maybe he was.

Hitler, Eva thought about him, Hitler. What was he like at home? He'd never married. She could be such a good wife to him, staunch and devoted, solid and clean. No frills in their house. She'd fantasized kissing him at the rally. Stop it, she told herself. Just stop it. There was a man selling pictures and post-cards of Hitler near the parish house when she got there. She stopped on her way in and bought some.

There was only one thing that perplexed Eva, and that was the Nazi attitude toward Lutheranism. She couldn't figure it out. Some parishioners said Nazism and Christianity would go hand in hand and together make a better Germany. Others warned the Nazis wanted to subvert the church and take it over. Eva didn't know, but she couldn't see how any party who held such glorious rallies could fail to understand God. The whole thing was a mistake. The Lutheran Church always participated in government—that was history—and the Nazis had ousted the Communist heathens. No. Hand in hand, that's what it would be, and, anyway, doing away with Christianity was an impossibility.

Eva walked down the hall of the parish house and into the white, sparsely furnished room where the meetings were held. Lotte, Emmie, and Berthe were sitting around the table as usual. They were all in their eighth month of pregnancy and all smug about it. Well, now Eva could be smug, too. They looked funny sitting there with their huge stomachs. They were talking about Hitler and how handsome they thought he was. She was about to agree when they suddenly shut up and stared at her. Emmie looked distinctly guilty.

"Hello," Eva said uncertainly.

"Hello," Emmie said weakly.

The others smiled falsely. There was no cake. There were no cries of "Happy birthday."

"Eva"—Lotte fiddled nervously with the brim of her hat—"sit down, dear, we have a little problem, but I'm sure it can be taken care of with your help."

"A problem?" Eva repeated.

She sat down.

"Yes," said Berthe. "Umm."

Berthe put one of her gloves on and tamped down the spaces between the fingers. She was searching for words.

"You must tender your resignation, dear. That's all there is to it," Lotte said.

"Why?" asked Eva, shocked. She looked at the others. Emmie looked away. Berthe stared at her coldly.

"Your ancestry, of course. You didn't tell us about your ancestry," said Berthe angrily.

"You're a Jew," said Lotte, accusing.

Emmie blushed.

"What are you talking about?" cried Eva. "I grew up in a Lutheran orphanage. I am baptized and confirmed. It's a lie. Who says I'm a Jew? It's one of those rumors, isn't it?"

"No," said Emmie kindly. "We got this letter from the orphanage. Your parents were Jewish, Eva, and because of the renewal process, of Nazification, we can't have anybody who's—"

"You're lying," said Eva and snatched the letter. "Oh, my God," she said when she'd read it. "Oh, my God."

"We could tell you to go, but, really, it would be best if you resigned. So much less . . ."

"Messy," finished Berthe.

"I'm sorry," said Emmie and lowered her eyes.

The others said nothing. They folded their arms and sat waiting for Eva to speak. She didn't. She just took up her purse and ran out of the room without looking back.

Eva stumbled out of the parish house and went home. When her husband came in that night and she told him she was pregnant and a Jew, they both wept, unable to make sense of such an inexplicable horror. For they both, if the truth were known, kept aloof from Jews, and the whole thing just made no sense to them. Eva contacted the orphanage and found that a set of files, including hers, had for thirty-five years been misplaced, only to be found during recent renovations done with funds provided by the new Nazi government. A Mr. and Mrs. Tannenbaum, killed in an automobile accident. No surviving relatives. She had been brought in by a Lutheran passerby.

In the two years that followed, Eva was ostracized by her church and community, and in the end the strain was too much for her marriage. Her husband divorced her and kept the baby and she went underground, hiding out in one vacant apartment after another, aided only by a young Catholic social worker who, before the war, Eva had distrusted because of her heresy.

Being a devout Lutheran, Eva continued to go to church in the center of Berlin where no one knew her. It seemed essential, as her belief was being tried, to convince God of her trust in Him. And she pondered her dilemma, desperate to make sense of it. It seemed she had Jewish blood, mongrel blood, flowing through her veins, bequeathed to her by Jewish parents she had never known.

The circle of nicotine addicts shifted in their chairs.

How this blood affected her, she couldn't fathom, since no one had ever noticed it, not she herself, or Lotte and Berthe, who knew everything about Jews and hated them. Day after day, she pondered her Jewish parents and what came to her mind were the drawings she'd seen in *Der Sturmer*: grotesque-looking people with huge noses and hairy bodies, and she couldn't fathom it at all.

Finally, in 1939, she was arrested. A locksmith who came to change the locks of the apartment in which she was hiding reported her because she spurned his advances. Eva died of typhus in Auschwitz soon after her arrival.

Eve lowered her eyes to indicate she was done and silence reigned. Then Tim blurted out, "Well, of course, next to that, this seems like bullshit."

"One man's bullshit," began Cathy, "another man's—"

"Tragedy," finished Bob.

VIII

Eve was lying on the bed watching the news. East Germany was beginning to crack. So many people had fled through the Hungarian corridor that the Communists were panicking. They were trying to stop the exodus, which was causing more demonstrations and pressure.

"The Communists are so dumb. How can they be so dumb?"

Eve addressed this to Charles César as he walked through the door. He looked at the TV.

"They live in prison and prison law is the law of the dumb," he said.

He took off his tie and hung it up.

"Are you going with me to Benny's party?" Eve asked.

"No," he replied.

Charles César had stuck to his resolve not to go out with her as long as she had the tattoo. They had not been out together in a month, nor had she made love with him. He seemed to be gripped by a strange emotion, a tortuous twist of tension and sorrow that kept him from anger but did not allow him to weep. When he took off his shirt and sat down on the bed, he just drooped.

"Please come," Eve asked.

Eve was also torn. She adored Charles César but she could not give up the tattoo. She viewed it now as her personal

salvation. Ever since she'd gotten it, truths had been coming out, truths that needed to come out, and at this time in her life, nothing was more important to her than that. Her alliance with 500123, the woman she called Eva, was the strongest bond she had ever formed. And though she felt for Charlie and could see the pain his past so obviously caused him, she resented his refusal to confide in her. And there was something else: his intensity of presence, what was it, his humanity, once so exciting, so enlivening, was beginning to embarrass her and she found it over the top.

"No," answered Charles César. "No. I cannot."

"What's going to happen? We're never going to go out again?"

"I don't know. I told you how I feel."

"We're never going to have sex again?" She asked this even though she knew she shouldn't.

He didn't reply. He gave her a cold look and put on a clean shirt.

"Well?"

"I think that's up to you." There was menace in his tone.

"This has nothing to do with me," Eve snapped. "This has to do with your parents!"

"I told you—" Charles César began and then stopped himself. He turned and made for the door.

"Wait a minute!" Eve shouted. "Just wait a minute!"

Charles César paused in the doorway and stared at her.

"You're always leaving, leaving in the middle of important things, like I might learn something from your absences, like I'm a naughty child who has to stay in solitary till she sees the light. The hell with your arrogance! The hell with it!"

"Ah, Eve," Charles César seemed crushed.

He sank onto the bed and Eve crawled over to him on her knees and put her arms around him.

"I love you so," she whispered in his ear.

She kissed his neck and inhaled him hungrily. She felt as if she were smelling sweet bread baking inside a closed bakery. He pulled away and got up.

"What was it you said once, 'Jews make the best lovers'?" He was looking down at her with a sadistic grin.

"I was only teasing you," she said and then realized what she'd said. "I told you that?"

She'd forgotten.

"Yes. You came home from lunch one day and told me that."

She remembered now. She'd been lunching with Alice and Cilla. She came home and threw herself into Charles César's arms. They kissed for what seemed like an hour. And then she drew back and, safe in the heat of his eyes, she teased, "Cilla and Alice say Jews make the best lovers."

"I said, 'Cilla and Alice say Jews make the best lovers.' But I added, thinking you were Catholic, 'They're wrong.' I don't remember what you said."

"I said they were right, of course." He laughed sarcastically.

"Listen, Charlie," she said. "I woke up one morning before my fortieth birthday and I felt like nothing and no one. I felt like I had everything I could possibly need and none of it meant anything. I felt like I lost my fire, you know. I couldn't think of a single place on the globe I wanted to travel to. I felt trapped.

"So I went back over my life and I started thinking about my first job. I was seventeen. I was a reader for a Broadway director who was consumed with the holocaust. He wanted to make a movie about it. He had me read everything I could get hold of on the subject. But the book I remember best was called *Night*, by a man called Hilsenrath."

"Don't tell me," Charles César said, "please."

"Listen. Just listen," she pleaded. "The book was about a Jewish middle-class man trying to survive in one of the ghettos the Nazis constructed. It's a chronicle of this man trying to survive from day to day, just trying to get food. The Nazis have destroyed everything he had, his family, his livelihood, his country, his values. Only his will to live persists. One scene stuck with me all these years: the man finally falls sick with typhus. He has hidden himself under a stairwell, trying to get peace, and someone, more debased by the Nazis than even he thought possible, comes along and, taking advantage of his weakness, pries the gold out of his teeth. While he is still alive. While he is still alive."

Charles César closed his eyes and sighed.

"And that book changed me," she went on. "Because it made the ghetto so real. It was modern. The Warsaw Ghetto had telephones, for God's sake. And this guy had been a business-man. And I had to ask myself: How did the Nazis get people to help them? And—specifically, How did the Nazis get women to help them?—Because it was women who kept Hitler going in Nazi Germany through the lean times. Women adored him. Women did his fund-raising. How did he get women, Christian women, to aid and abet him in mass murder? You see this—" Eve gestured at the TV, at the demonstrations in East Germany and Czechoslovakia that were flashing on the screen. Charles César looked at the TV.

"This is all about the Nazis. It took forty years to get over the cataclysm they caused, to get over the cruelty people inflicted on each other. I often wonder whether Eastern Europeans and Russians put up with totalitarianism for so long because they felt they deserved it after what they saw and did during the Nazi period. A kind of penance. Fifty-five million people died in the Second World War, think of it, fifty-five million people."

Eve and Charlie focused on the TV, where thousands of Czechs were screaming for freedom.

"What about the men?" Charlie asked.

"Well, of course, men, too. But the tattoo's not about men. It's about the hearts and souls of women. About me. I'm of German ancestry. I'm a Christian. I'm a woman and I have to know—do I have mass murder in my blood or what?"

"For Christ's sake, Eve," Charlie shouted.

"I thought you were Catholic. I thought we could explore the Christian part together. I didn't know—"

"Can we ever stop talking about the fucking Nazis!" He hissed this.

"Yes," Eve said quietly. "But first I must tell you two things, 51 two clues I found, and then we'll think about them and discuss them another time, okay? Please? Please?"

"Okay," Charlie sighed so deeply she thought he might pass out.

"Okay. We're investigating mass murder. That's what everyone knows about: the mass gassing of Jews in the camps, innocent, ordinary people. My question is, How did women make this palatable to themselves, Christian women? Okay? Clue number one is the Euthanasia Program. The first mass gassing of innocent human beings involved non-Jewish mental patients in an asylum outside of Berlin. Clue number two is these laws from the Racial Hygiene program I'm going to read to you.

Eve got up and ran to her stack of Nazi books and retrieved one called *Racial Hygiene*. "Listen," she said, and began to read.

" 'July fourteenth, 1933, Sterilization Law: forcible sterilizations for anyone with the following conditions in their family: feeblemindedness, schizophrenia, manic-depression, epilepsy, Huntington's chorea, genetic blindness or deafness, alcoholism.

" 'November twenty-fourth, 1933, Castration Law: castration of career criminals and sex offenders.

" 'September fifteenth, 1935, Marriage Health Law: barred marriage or sex between non-Jews and Jews.

" 'November fifteenth, 1935, Citizenship Law: which distinguished "citizens," ' "—that's non-Jewish Germans—'from "inhabitants," Jews obviously, but also *unmarried non-Jewish women*.'

"That one's my personal favorite, of course. Unmarried Aryan women were not citizens of the Reich after 1935, thank you. That means Eva Braun, you know.

"Now, understand that these were laws, not attitudes, not beliefs, laws—and we'll mull that over and I'll get back to you."

"Listen to me." Charles César came over to the bed and stood above her.

"Oh, I forgot one thing," Eve said. " 'Thirty-nine is the beginning date for the Euthanasia Program. 'Thirty-nine."

"Eve, I can't take this," Charlie said. "I can't hear about it. I don't want to mull it over. I can't take it."

He stared down at his girlfriend. All trace of Donna Reed had vanished. It was frightening. He moved toward the door.

"Where are you going?" Eve asked.

"Out," he replied.

"You have Benny's address?"

"I'm not going to Benny's. I'm not going anywhere with you as long as you have that tattoo. Especially," he added, "to bed."

She sat back and stared mindlessly at the TV. The head of East Germany was making some dumb speech, trying to persuade fleeing Communists to stay at home—things would get better.

"Call me Anastasia," she barked at the TV.

"Good-bye, Anastasia," said Charles César, not getting the joke, and he left the room.

IX

The security man at the door had trouble finding her name.

"There it is," she pointed to it on the sheet of paper. "There it is."

She and Charles César were listed together. The security man looked up, expecting to see him by her side.

"He's not coming," Eve said. "He's got flu."

Behind her, the fiction editor of a powerful magazine shuffled up drunkenly, encircled by several pilot-fish first novelists. Eve nodded to them, gave her wrap to the very young person checking coats in the lobby, and entered the elevator. The fiction editor and novelists lurched in behind her. She turned, encountered them face to face, and smiled. Benny's party was for Talmadge Weehawken's second novel. As his first had been financially and halfway literarily successful, the evening promised to bring out every suck in the book business.

"Moluk is a damn fine writer," the fiction editor was mumbling. "One of the best damn craftsmen of, hell, the twentieth century."

The first novelists bobbed their heads up and down in agreement. Eve had the distinct impression that they were treading water around him. The fiction editor was referring to a man who wrote one novel every twenty years. When it came out, though unreadable, it was always thought to be a perfect book, and its author was roundly praised primarily because he had stayed at home for nineteen years and hadn't offended anyone. No human Eve had ever met had ever read anything by him.

"What's his new book about?" she asked.

The fiction editor looked blank. Then he said, "Man's search for the miraculous," quoting the newspaper Sunday review.

The first novelists oohed with respect at his erudition.

"The miraculous what?" Eve asked, but they had reached Benny's door and they all escaped inside before he had to answer.

There were about twenty people already there, and the pressure was building. Across the room, Talmadge and Benny were talking to some development women from a major movie studio. Talmadge was hoping for a big movie sale and, even this far away, Eve could see he was shamelessly flattering one, probably the more powerful one, of the women.

Eve had read Talmadge's book. It was accomplished but a bit odd. He was obsessed with the breeding of afghans and this was the second book in which afghans figured as a subplot. Eve had found it interesting, but the *New York Times* critic had been sardonic. And when the *Times* critic was sardonic, agents and publishers wept, editors poo-pooed it, and writers went on a binge. It would be a great party.

"Congratulations, Talmadge. I loved the book." Eve kissed him on both cheeks and stood back, exhausted by the effort.

"Benny, hi," she added and kissed him twice, too. Doubly exhausted.

"Eve. You look lovely," Talmadge said, barely meaning it.

Eve turned to the development women. "Don't you just love this book?" Eve smiled at them dumbly. She was pretending she didn't know who they were.

"Eve," the less powerful one said, "we've met. Amy Werner?"

"Of course. I'm sorry."

"And this is Betty Bern."

"Hi."

Eve turned to the more powerful one and extended her hand first. Thus, the more powerful one knew she, too, was powerful.

"God," Eve cried, "I love your shoes. Maud Frizon?"

Powerful but feminine, capable of good gossip.

"Robert Clergerie."

The more powerful one dropped the French shoe designer's name like a gauntlet.

"My favorite," Eve whispered throatily.

Talmadge's book had been forgotten. The men were left in the dust.

"The round-toed black suede pump with the Louis Quinze heels?"

The more powerful one sighed deeply in assenting appreciation. "I know your work, Eve," she purred. "I love it."

Eve thanked her. She probably did know Eve's work. Women in development usually did read women's writing. It assuaged their guilt for not buying it. Men's writing they only perused, but they bought it for their companies. They never read it. It bored them stiff.

Talmadge was desperately trying to win back the women's attention.

"What do you think of my shoes?" he asked boyishly, sticking out one cordovan loafer.

A neurotic young starlet appeared at this moment, very beautiful, a little drunk.

"Talmadge," she said, "has one foot in the preppie world, another on a banana peel."

The women laughed hysterically. The actress drifted away. Eve sought to return Talmadge to his evening's pedestal.

"Talmadge's use of the historical present in that book was masterful," Eve said soberly.

The women didn't really know what she meant, but they nodded wisely. They were in development after all. They didn't need to know, only to suspect.

"I think he has a very visual mind," Eve added.

Talmadge was blushing. The two women started going back to work, praising and petting him. Eve was just turning away when the less powerful one spotted the tattoo.

"Is that from the sixties?" she asked.

Eve froze. What could the woman be talking about, she thought. Is she saying I look forty? Then she saw the woman was pointing at the tattoo.

"Oh," Eve looked down at her forearm. She felt sick with guilt. She had forgotten about Eva.

"Is that from the sixties?" the less powerful one repeated.

"No," Eve replied. "It's the prisoner I.D. number of a woman who died in the Nazi camps. Her name was Eva Berg."

"Oh, God. Are you in a play or a movie or something?" The less powerful one was probing now.

"No. I'm wearing it in remembrance. That's all."

The more powerful one, who seemed to be deep in conversation with Benny and Talmadge, suddenly swiveled her head around and asked, "Will you be writing about that when you're done wearing it?" She glanced meaningfully at the less powerful one.

"No," said Eve.

"No?"

The development women shuddered imperceptibly. There was something just a little bit offensive to them about people who had experiences and didn't make book on them. It was a little too earthy for them to bear.

"You should," the less powerful one said.

"Yes," the more powerful one agreed.

"Nice to see you," Eve said and sauntered away to the bar.

The two development women watched her walk away. They were very concerned. The starlet, who had focused on the scene from afar, came up and asked, "What's wrong? What happened?"

"She's got the prisoner number of a Nazi camp victim tattooed on her arm," the less powerful one said.

57

"And she's not writing about it," the more powerful one finished.

"Damn, I wish I'd thought of that!" The starlet stamped her foot.

A bar had been set up in one corner of Benny's apartment. Eve got herself over to it and ordered a stiff gin and tonic. She was shaken. She had forgotten about Eva. The minute she had set foot in the apartment, she had been drawn into the dance. Now she felt tainted again and as if she had betrayed Eva.

Two boy publishers, who were lounging at the end of the bar, walked over to her and inquired about Charlie.

"Oh, he's home," she lied. "He's got flu."

"You look beautiful tonight, Eve. He shouldn't let you out by yourself," the older of the two said.

Eve was surprised. This was a compliment on her work, but she couldn't recall what article might be out or where. It was an odd thing about the boy publishers that they were unable to say to her "great piece" or "I laughed a lot" or the usual flatteries they said to male writers. It was easier for them to speak about her eyes or her waist or her general sensuality.

"How small *is* your waist?" the younger one asked, placing his hands around it.

"Oh, 'Ceausescu's Budget Tips,' " Eve remembered.

The boy publishers laughed. One gave her a squeeze. As she wasn't one of their authors, neither boy felt it necessary to discuss the strange black numbers tattooed on her arm.

Eve finished her drink, got another from the bartender, and made her way toward a clump of treelike editors slouching together by an open window.

They were giving her an odd look as she approached and just beyond them she could see the development women scurrying away to the front door where Oliver Stone, the movie director, was making his entrance preceded almost by a flourish of trumpets.

The three editors seemed to be swaying together in the

breeze. Eve had known them all since her first writing days in New York, fifteen years by this time, and they hadn't changed much, just gotten less fiery and a bit grizzled around the edges. They were all drinking heavily. To Eve's knowledge, there were no editors in recovery around the city. They simply refused to recover. They took that as one of their prerogatives.

They were all married to women they'd dated for years. They all had new babies. They regarded Eve in her childless, fortyish state on a continuum from tragedy to temptation depending on the evening. As the development women had told them about the tattoo, tonight they regarded her with actual interest.

"Hello, Evie, what are you up to?" Frank, the thinnest one, clapped her on the back. He did want to know.

"Watching TV, that's all I do. Watching Eastern Europe go free. Isn't it wonderful? Did you ever think in our lifetime—"

"You're lucky you can stay home and watch it." Bill, the fat one, was irked.

"That's the beautiful thing about America: you can sit home and scribble down your thoughts and make a living at it. I'd never be good at factory work though. If war comes, I won't be of much use."

"Hey, you got a tattoo!" Curt, the athletic one, took her arm and looked at it closely.

"What is it with the Communists that they don't understand that in a global economy, people want to travel?" Eve was trying to change the subject. The atmosphere around her was so false, she wasn't sure if she wanted to tell a tale. She wasn't ready. "Can you imagine being forced to stay in New York City all your life?"

"Yes, I can," said Bill. "I can't afford to go anywhere else. And I can't afford to stay here. Capitalism is another kind of hell."

"Well, then. I certainly won't be selling you any automatic weapons," Eve said.

"No, don't," replied Bill. "I could open up on a subway car any morning."

"Fax the president, won't you, Bill?" said Eve.

"Yeah," agreed Curt, "he refuses to admit how deeply wacked the average joe is."

"Free but wacked," agreed Frank.

"How are the kids?" Eve asked them all.

The men smiled warmly. Each had behaved badly during the pregnancy of his wife and each had fallen in love with the baby that was subsequently born, and each had turned into a fairly upstanding character in the end. Eve was proud of their entrance into adulthood even if they did look a bit moth-eaten.

"So what's with the tattoo, Eve?"

Frank asked the direct question and the other editors stood waiting, unabashedly, for her answer. The fact that she had put them off once before made no difference to them. Eve was struck by the fact that, with respect to their curiosity, male editors were extraordinarily like women. They were extremely simpatico in matters of love, and prone to feeling left out. There was a sweet quality to them that let her know that they'd never screw her in business unless their jobs were truly on the line.

"It's the I.D. number of an Auschwitz prisoner named Eva Berg."

The editors examined her forearm.

"Boy, it's ugly, isn't it?" said Curt. "It's like a bruise."

"Gives me the chills. Get rid of it, Eve. It's horrifying," said Bill.

"Why did you get it?" asked Frank.

"I'm a WASP. I feel guilt by association with the cruel and brutal Aryans who aided and abetted mass murder."

"I never thought of it in that way," said Frank. "Are you cruel and brutal?"

"I have been in moments of my life, haven't you?"

Eve looked at the three editors, and they blushed and lowered their eyes. They had never seen her be cruel and brutal but she had seen them. She had seen them at parties like this one with their pregnant wives. She had seen the wives watch with dumb pain as the men they depended on publicly drooled over younger, thinner women. The wives, standing there, horrified, involuntarily turning into bowling pins.

When the babies were born, they became again loving men, respectful men, and all was forgotten. But Eve had seen them defiant and cruel and she knew they had it in them.

But, perhaps, she thought, in the world of men, this was not such a big crime. Not as big a crime, say, as wearing a tattoo in public that shamed your man and made him impotent.

"You're of the we-all-have-it-in-us-school, then?" Frank asked.

"No, I'm not actually. Like Anne Frank, I believe that people are basically good at heart."

Bill made a derisive sound.

"I do. I mean that. I think there has to be more to it than just inherent sadism. I believe there was more to it than that."

"What?" asked Frank.

"Well," began Eve, "did you know that the Nazis first developed their mass gassing techniques, the forging of death certificates, the whole grisly mechanism of killing and lying, for use on Aryan Germans?"

"No," said Frank. "I didn't."

"Yes," she went on, "under something called the Euthanasia Program. They wanted to do away with mentally defective Germans. The plan was to get rid of the alcoholic, the schizophrenic, the chronically depressed—"

"All of New York City was eligible," said Bill.

They all laughed gratefully.

"Yes," Eve said. "So, first they gassed the weak members of their own so-called race and lied to their families."

"That's quite amazing," said Frank.

"Isn't it? And, of course, at the same time, they made it easier to institutionalize people."

"I knew there had to be some good in the Nazis," said Bill.

"Look"—Eve ignored him—"I think Lanzmann proved in

his film *Shoah* that many people knew what was happening to the Jews. They knew through the workers on the train system. Before 'forty-one, they knew the Jews were being sent to camps. Then when the gassing started, they heard about that, if only through rumor. The train system was *the* method of transport then, virtually the only method."

"Okay," said Frank, "so?"

"So, why didn't they protest the gassing of Jews and why didn't they fear for themselves?"

"They were virulent anti-Semites, Eve," said Frank with exasperation.

"To be virulently anti-Semitic doesn't mean you approve of mass murder," Eve replied. "And anyone who is constantly seeing masses of people arrested and hunted around him is bound to feel nervous for himself and his family. Why didn't they fear for themselves?"

"They thought they were invincible," Bill said. "Everybody knows that."

"Yes," said Eve, "that's one explanation. But the only one? Can it be the only one?"

"I have wondered about that," said Frank. "At the very least I'd fear my child might get caught in a crossfire or rounded up by mistake."

"And what about your wife?" Eve asked. "How would she feel?"

"She'd be hysterical about it. She can't stand violence," he replied.

"Okay. Now here's something else. In 1933, the year Hitler came to power, he instituted the Sterilization Law. The so-called mentally defective were to be forcibly sterilized. Alcoholics, depressives—do you have any idea how many people that could involve?"

"Certainly most of Akron, Ohio," said Curt.

"And St. Paul, Minnesota," said Frank.

"What gender is most often hospitalized for depression?"

The men stared at Eve.

"That's right," she said, "women."

"The Nazis were monsters. The Germans were monsters," Curt said. "Thank God we took away their army and divided their country. God knows what's going to happen with the wall coming down. Tell us about your tattoo, Eve. Let's get off this. Who was Eva Berg?"

Eve looked down at the number on her forearm and then up at the party around her. The drunken starlet was perched on the knee of a novelist in his mid-forties who was talking loudly about his absent wife. Moluk had arrived and the first novelists were genuflecting before him as he spoke delightedly about a black kid who had tried to sell him crack and with whom he talked Kafka. In the corner, the fiction editor was hovering over a celebrated literary couple like a giant crow over a shiny bauble. The female of the couple was saying, "So I went to Fred Segal to try and get something to wear to the Oscars. I felt I was representing the literary community and I should look smart, no? But all they had were bras studded with spikes. So militaristic, this modern sexuality."

The fiction editor laughed uproariously as did the development women who, when they heard the word *Oscars*, immediately homed in like pigeons to their roost.

Eve ran her finger over the tattoo and began, "Eva Berg was a gynecologist in Berlin when the Nazis came to power, a gynecologist and obstetrician."

At this the men relaxed. They all knew obstetricians and had worked with them in delivery rooms.

"Eva had obtained her degree at the height of the suffragette movement in Weimar, Germany. She had thought she would dedicate her life to the eradication of certain female diseases that she was studying in the laboratory adjacent to her office. She had planned on it, in fact. So it came as a great shock to her when the Nazis got in, and, in 1933, stripped women of the rights they had won, outlawed birth control, instituted a whole raft of invasive laws, and made the performing of abortions a treasonable offense. Through no fault of her own, Eva, an upstanding citizen, suddenly became a fighter on the female front lines."

The day she was arrested in 1940, Eve continued, began as did most of her days. She spent the morning at Hereditary Health Court. As an Aryan doctor, she was empowered to defend against any sterilizations proposed under the Law for the Prevention of Hereditarily Diseased Offspring. The law stated that anyone suffering from feeblemindedness, schizophrenia, manic-depression, genetic epilepsy, Huntington's chorea, blindness, deafness, or severe alcoholism was a candidate for forcible sterilization. Doctors could defend against it but they also had to recommend candidates, and she spent some part of her precious time trying to weasel out, claiming she was too busy to fill out the papers or that they got lost in the mail. Fortunately, and to her, inexplicably, many people volunteered to be sterilized out of some bizarre patriotism to the Reich, and she often fiddled with their papers, changing their volunteerism into her recommendation, and that got her off the hook.

That morning's defense involved Harry Weber, the husband of her friend Maria. Sometime after Kristallnacht, Harry, who was a sensitive, gentle man, began to drink. He had been out on the street during the roundup of Jews and had gotten a black eye trying to protect an old woman who was being beaten by the SS. Whatever else he saw that night, he refused to discuss when he returned home, his face and hands bloodied from flying glass, his eye swollen like a melon. He just drank a schnapps, and then another after that, and he hadn't been sober since.

Harry came afoul of the law when he fell down a flight of steps in a public park and was taken to hospital. He had only sprained his ankle, but his drunkenness was noticed as was his depressed state, and the hospital director informed Harry's local medical officer, who looked into the matter.

Harry's neighbors were interviewed, his coworkers and students, as well as the neighbors and coworkers of his parents and grandparents. And it was discovered that Harry's father and grandfather both frequented the beer halls and had been known for the raucousness of their Saturday nights. Harry was, thereby, deemed a "hereditary and chronic alcoholic" and recommended for sterilization. His depression, thank God, could not be proved to be hereditary, and so there was no danger of his being hospitalized in an institution.

"Thank God for small favors," Maria had said through her tears.

Very large favors, Eva thought, but did not say it. The trouble had been bad enough.

Witnesses who had seen Harry help the Jewish woman on Kristallnacht testified in court, and so Eva lost the case. She never could believe how many people were willing to testify to others' weaknesses. They seemed to have no sense of their own vulnerability at all. It was true that when the Reich deemed you a miscreant, you pretty much lost your credibility; still, people were reeducated and reclaimed, and twice she had seen revenge taken at court. Witnesses against those who had witnessed against them smiled with such pleasure.

Harry had been no help. When accused of helping Jews, he cried out, "No! Being Christian!" which enraged the judge who ruled, instantly, for sterilization.

At the verdict, Maria broke down sobbing. She and Harry had only one, rather sickly child, and now, not only were they branded by the state as inferior, but they would have no other children, a further societal shame. As for Harry, he was led away with a terrible look on his face. Like a male cat being handed to the veterinarian for castration.

The three editors looked a bit green, but they were hanging on her every word. Eve continued.

So that was Eva's morning. She got back to her office around noon and ate lunch at her desk alone. As she often did after one of these jarring experiences at Hereditary Health Court, she 65 ruminated on her life in medicine. If, she thought, she could figure out how to preserve human spermatazoa for later insemination, she could save people so much pain. It could be done, of course, but it would take research and time and money, none of which she had now that her every moment was taken up with hysterical women pleading for HHC defenses, illegal abortions, and falsified marriage certificates swearing racial soundness. There was one good thing about it all: women were hardly ill anymore. She hadn't seen a simple urinary infection in months.

What Eva could not quite reconcile in her mind was that she had become a criminal. On a daily basis now, almost without thought, she lied and performed acts that were punishable by imprisonment. Well, the Nazi laws were interminable. Every day there was a new one more convoluted than the last, with more paperwork for doctors, and more suffering for the average woman. Not for every woman. No, if you were a racially sound breeder, then fine. Although a breeder of females was not so good. How many times had she been asked—Do you have the recipe for conceiving sons? Reichsführer SS Himmler was said to know how this was done. Eva laughed to herself. There had been something in the Reich Mothers' Service news about it, some fool wives' tale from the Swabian Alps.

What was she to do? Just yesterday another desperate girl had appeared in her office who had an ancestress back in 1860 who had married a Jew. The day before there was a girl with a retarded brother, and one whose grandfather was a manic-depressive. The Marriage Health Law of 1935 stated that those with infectious or hereditary diseases could not marry. Since the Nazis had deemed Judaism, mongolism, and manic-depression to be hereditary diseases, these women were doomed to spinsterhood and loss of citizenship without her help. She signed their Certificates of Suitability for Marriage without a thought.

For in addition to forcing her to commit fraud, the Marriage Law had made her nights a living hell of concealment and subterfuge. How many stillbirths with severe birth defects had she buried in cemeteries around the city, eradicating all evidence of their nonexistence lest their mothers be subject to sterilization? Her life had become a parody of Burke and Hare. The Certificates of Suitability for Marriage, well, they were just the tip of her iceberg.

At one o'clock, Eva had office visits. The three afternoon hours during which Eva tended mostly pregnant women represented the only normalcy left to her, and she relished them. Today she had Frau Keller, winner of the Mother's Cross in gold for her production of eight hereditarily perfect, healthy children. Eva had fifteen such winners as patients, ten silver winners for six children apiece, and five bronze for four. Because of her exceptional prenatal care and medical skill in bringing so many healthy babies to term, Eva was well regarded by the state. Ironically she had a sterling reputation.

As the last patient waddled out the door, Eva began to prepare for the rest of her day. She closed up the front of her office, drew the shades, locked the door, and retreated to the back rooms where she began to take out the tools with which she performed abortions. Her servant, Heidi, aided her in this criminal endeavor, and as the back doorbell pealed, Heidi shuffled off to let the pale, shuddering women come in from the alley.

The first patient was Bette Reiner, machinist at the I. G. Farben chemical plant outside the city. Bette's husband had been called up in '39 and during a recent home visit had made Bette pregnant. Until her husband had left for the army, Bette had been a housewife living happily on her husband's wages and the bonus reichsmarks she received for having five children. She held, of course, a bronze Mother's Cross.

But as soon as her husband was gone, the state decreed that women, even mothers of five, should go back to work to aid the war effort. Bette had a hard time with this. She had come to Eva several times in a frantic state. It was not the plant work she minded, it was being separated from her children. She felt horribly guilty.

Eva felt sympathy for her. Before the war the state had

mounted a massive campaign against mothers working. Posters showing the evils that would befall children whose mothers worked hung everywhere, even in Eva's own office. It was part of the state effort to get women out of the work force. Bette had been propagandized.

Now, a few short years later, posters proclaiming the glory of women working for victory and Führer had replaced their opposites, and women like Bette were in turmoil. Though the hideous things that might befall her children were no longer mentioned, Bette experienced them in her nightmares. When she discovered she was pregnant, she had a breakdown.

Eva placed Bette on a bed in the laboratory and kept her there until she was better. This was the way Eva now dealt with all mental problems affecting her patients. She dared not risk them to the mental wards of hospitals, not with the forced sterilizations and the Euthanasia Program, no.

When Bette was ambulatory again, she again begged Eva for an abortion. Her reasoning, a crazy mixmatch of propaganda and paranoia, was that, left at home in the care of others, the new infant might turn Jewish and poison the family. Eva consented. It was obvious that Bette would never be able to leave the infant and go to work without complete mental disintegration. She was capable of killing the infant in her present condition. The state had done its work well. It was undoing its work that was Eva's continuing burden.

Bette arrived in a haze of false cheer. She was rather dressed up for such an occasion, even wearing her bronze Mother's Cross. Eva told her to disrobe and put on a cotton gown in the dressing room, and then come back when she was ready. While Eva waited, she rehearsed in her thoughts what she would tell the judge if she were ever arrested.

"Can you imagine, gentlemen, that a woman might come before the state? That the carrying of a creature inside one's womb might entitle one to some say in the matter?" This last, of course, she would say only to herself. Whether she wanted to die for women's suffrage was a question she preferred not to ask herself before a procedure.

Bette came back in and got on the table and put her feet in the stirrups. While Heidi administered the anesthetic, Eva gazed at Bette's body. It was ruined, that was the word for it. Ruined. Her stomach was like a sagging bag that hung limply from her waist. Her breasts were withered and mottled. She was criss-crossed by stretch marks, like knife wounds. Inside, she was a mess of scar tissue. The last two had been forceps births. There had also been a breech. Eva had done the best she could.

The fact was Bette's body couldn't take it. The body wasn't up to five pregnancies in a row and more to come. Nor was her hormonal system. It had reached the breaking point, if it had not already broken. Eva felt guilty as she prepared Bette for the surgery. She and her husband used French letters, which she got from a doctor friend in France. She wished she could give them to all her patients, but she could only get enough for herself.

She was in the middle of the curettage when the Gestapo started pounding on the door. She gestured to Heidi to sit quietly and do nothing while she calmly and methodically finished up just as they smashed in the door glass. Bette was, of course, under general anesthesia, and so mercifully ignorant of the proceedings.

By the time the Gestapo entered the operating chamber, Eva had disposed of the fetal tissue, secreting it in a carved-out hollow inside a copy of Nietzsche's works, which she stuck in the bookcase.

The Gestapo got her anyway. The mental ward in the lab was discovered. Other patients she had aborted bore witness against her. The investigation had begun because the block warden on her street, a woman who had always received free obstetrical care, turned her in. Eva had told the woman that her menopause had started and it was unlikely that she was still fertile.

Eva was taken off to Gestapo Headquarters. She was interrogated and tortured, then tried, convicted, and sentenced to twenty years in prison. Because of the sensitive nature of her crimes and their collision course with the Nazi Racial Program, her offenses were considered political and treasonable, and she was sent to a series of concentration camps instead. She died in the gas chamber at Auschwitz in 1943 after she was found performing abortions for Jewish prisoners forced to work in brothels, or who had been raped by camp guards.

Bette and the other women the Gestapo found at the clinic were arrested and kept at the central prison just long enough for Bette to go certifiably insane and the others to be forcibly sterilized. Bette was sent to a mental institution where she died in a mass gassing under the Euthanasia Program in 1941. Her family was told she died of pneumonia.

Eve finished her tale and looked down at the tattoo. The three editors sighed sadly and stared at it, too.

"Jesus," Frank said.

The more powerful of the development women who had been, literally, lurking nearby, leaned in and said desperately, "Don't you want to write that down, Eve? Just on a three-by-five card or something, not a whole treatment, and I could pitch it when the boss comes in this week? I'm sorry—I listened—okay? But it was brilliant and it's got everything: the women's angle, the thriller stuff. The abortion business is a little dicey and I'm not sure she should be a gynecologist—we usually reserve that for comedy—but—"

"How about a book?" Curt asked.

"No," said Eve, "no."

And she bid them good-bye and said good night to Talmadge and Benny and went home to watch TV.

X

Charles César left Eve on the morning the Berlin Wall fell. It was Saturday, November 10, and all week events in East Germany had been building to a climax. Erich Honecker, the Communist Party leader who had supervised the building of the wall in '61, and who had recently been deposed, was being charged with corruption and embezzling party coffers. There had been an attempt to close off the stream of emigration to the West, which resulted in riots. Finally, on November 9, the East German government announced the opening of all its borders, including the Berlin Wall.

Eve had stayed up as late as she could on Friday night, but actually she had fallen asleep early. Charles César had been out, as he always was now, and Eve had been unable to keep awake, she felt, so she wouldn't have to see him when he came home.

When she awoke on Saturday morning, she turned on the TV and what she saw moved her to tears: hundreds of thousands of East German young people were playing with the Berlin Wall, scaling it, dancing on top of it, hitting and chipping at it with hammers. They reminded Eve of illustrations of shoemakers in German fairy tales.

"Charlie!"

She could hear him moving about in the next room.

"Come here and look. A whole nation doing performance art."

Charlie came in and sat on the bed close to the TV. "My God," he said, and against all his instincts, he smiled.

Eve began to cry.

"People feeling freedom are so beautiful, aren't they?" she said. "This is so moving."

Charles César stared dumbly at the TV and did not reply.

His small but aristocratic hands fidgeted with the bedcovers. Something about the shape of his head reminded her that he was foreign and she should never mistake the difference. He had eaten rations as a child, played soccer instead of baseball. And art was to him an entity as sacred as peanut butter. He was different. Maybe it was his carriage that made him look clerical, straight as a rod but relaxed, as if self-confidence were his birthright.

After a time of watching the young Germans frolic on the wall, he turned around and faced her. "I'm leaving, Eve," he said softly. "I'm packing now."

As Eve was already crying, an odd thing happened. Down in the pit of her stomach, the emotion prompting the tears feathered from joy to anguish in a physically painful rout. On the outside she appeared exactly the same.

"Forgive me," he went on, getting up, moving about the room, gathering his possessions. He gestured at the tattoo. "I can't live with that and you must, so *c'est ça.*"

"*Oui,*" agreed Eve sarcastically. "*C'est ça.*"

"Ah, Eve," he said with frustration.

"Where are you going?" she asked matter-of-factly.

"Over to Marc and Cilla's for a while and after that, I'm not sure."

Eve laughed to herself. Despite all their wars, the Europeans stuck together. Having hated each other so much made them almost incestuous in the end. Over the centuries they had bored deeply into each other's psyches down to that place where hate is indistinguishable from love. They were inseparable.

"That makes sense," she said.

On the TV screen, a young man, tightrope-walking on the wall, was offering a glass of wine to an equally young border guard. The guard took it and bowed in thanks. Then he drank it down. The crowd cheered.

"Look at that!" Eve whooped.

"It's incredible," said Charles César thoughtfully. "So sweet. I would never have expected them to be this sweet."

"No," Eve agreed. "One doesn't think of Eastern European Communists as being young and sweet. It's not the first thing that comes to mind."

Eve slumped into silence. She withdrew into the pillows and surveyed the bedroom that she and Charles César had put together. It was Chinoise in concept. The walls were dove gray. The TV sat at the end of the bed on a black lacquer table. The carpeting was gray with black specks. In one corner reclined a long, low black lacquer dresser that they shared, topped by a single pink peony in a gray vase. In another corner towered her stack of Nazi books, hidden, as Charles César had insisted, under an embroidered Chinese cloth. Along one wall stood closets fronted with black lacquer doors. Instead of curtains, Chinese paper screens closed silently over the big loft windows. There was nothing else in the room except the photo of Eva, propped up, in spite of Charles César, against the window screens, and a fire-engine red Calder mobile. Due to the furniture, which was Chinese antique, and the mobile, the room had a warm quality and a fifties arty flair.

Charles César opened the closets. Eve watched him closely as he began to pack.

"Don't go." She blurted this out in a high-pitched little-girl voice that surprised them both.

He came over to the bed, put his arms around her, and hugged her for a long time. His cheek was wet against her neck. When he raised his head, his eyes were red and swimming in sorrow.

"You give me no choice," he said and got up and returned to the closet. With his back to her, he took something from a high shelf and secreted it in his suitcase.

Eve glanced at the TV. The cameras had cut away from the wall now and were showing stores in West Germany beseiged by ogling East Germans.

They're going to want it all now, she thought, the Gucci shoes, the Hermès scarves, the BMWs and convertible Rabbits, the Maclaren strollers. Pretty soon they wouldn't be able to live without them. Pretty soon they'd be contemplating suicide if they couldn't afford them or holding an Uzi to their bank manager's head. Pretty soon they would no longer quote from the doctrines and dogmas, no longer remember who wrote them, no longer care. Pretty soon Milan Kundera and Yevtushenko and Havel would be writing boring, minimalist novels about the wages of too much freedom. No longer banned and dangerous, they'd be fighting for a reading audience and failing in a no-win competition with the Nintendo game.

"Freedom is a Faustian gift," she said out loud.

"If you believe life imitates Goethe, which I do not," said Charles César. "Freedom is an absolute. It has no detractions."

"Spoken like a European dreamer and former colonist," Eve said. "I know you will begrudge my saying this, but only Americans really know about freedom because, in this world, only we have it. In Western Europe, you have social bondage, family bondage, which keeps you in line. Here, we have utter freedom—the freedom even to destroy ourselves and the society and the environment and the soul—"

"Well, they have that in Asia."

"No, in Asia, they have terrible poverty and too many people."

"Your definition of freedom is absurd."

"No, it's just not romantic. Aging is the only prison Americans fear. Should we go to prison, the book and movie rights to our story will bring us freedom in immortality."

Charles César was getting angry.

"Ridiculous!" he snapped.

"Have it your way," Eve replied.

The TV was showing the Berlin Wall again, this time the Brandenburg Gate and Checkpoint Charlie, the famous border crossing, scene of infamous escapes and ugly cold-war standoffs.

As the program flashed old footage of incidents at the Wall, Eve's mind flashed on the places she'd been when she first saw them: her parents' living room, her grandparents' TV room, her first apartment, her second apartment. Now on the TV, there was Kennedy saying, *"Ich bin ein Berliner,"* for the two hundred millionth time, still handsome, still lovable, still alive. Eve had, she realized, a whole lifetime of personal associations with this wall she never thought about. Deep in her memory bank, this wall figured big. Before she was born, her father had flown in the Berlin airlift. Perhaps that, too, had affected her. Perhaps that's why she always liked foreign men.

Her eyes welled up with tears.

"I never thought I'd see this in my life, did you?"

"These are your Germans," Charles César said coldly, "the people responsible for that tattoo on your arm, and no, I prayed I wouldn't."

"Why do you hate the Germans so? It's not even your hatred, is it?"

"Forget it, Eve," Charlie was warning her.

She persisted.

"You know what?"

She sat up on the bed.

"You're leaving me because you hate the Germans."

"No." He spat this out. "I'm leaving you because you don't respect me!"

Eve was shocked.

"I do respect you. Of course I do. I didn't get the tattoo because I don't respect you. I didn't know how you'd feel."

"But you do now. You've known for months how I hate it and it's made no difference to you at all."

75

"That's not true," she said softly. "It has. But it's the Nazis you're angry about, not me, not the tattoo."

He stopped communicating with her and continued to pack.

She watched him, then the TV, and after a long time she said, "Look at these Germans. They're young kids. Maybe it's not fair to make them pay for the rest of their lives—"

"So get rid of the tattoo," he snapped.

"The tattoo is not there to embarrass you or the teenage Germans. It's to keep Eva alive, to remember Eva. Don't get confused."

Charles César slammed his suitcase shut and locked it. He set it upright on the floor, stared at Eve for a moment, then picked it up and left the room.

"Charlie, wait!"

Eve leapt off the bed and followed him to the front door.

"Please try and understand," she said when she got to him. "I need Eva. I need her."

Charles César was as wide-eyed and sorrowful and as French as she'd ever seen him. Alien. An alien being. Then his eyes narrowed.

"I'll send you a check at the end of the month," he said.

"You would talk about money now," she replied.

"Why? Because I'm a Jew?"

"You're so preoccupied with money. I don't even think about money. I wouldn't mention money at a time like—"

"You're crazy about money, Eve. You've got money and you don't pay your bills. How many times have the lights been turned off because you won't open your mail?"

"Why don't you see your parents? Because of money?"

He lunged forward and pushed her out of his way. She stuck out her forearm and shoved the tattoo at his eyes.

"Face it," she shouted.

Trembling, he set down his case, unlocked the locks, and opened the door.

"So long, little cabbage," he said in French, using that odd, loving diminutive.

XI

Several days after Charlie left, the phone rang at a time he usually called, and Eve rushed to pick it up.

"Hello," she said breathlessly. "Oh, hi, Dad."

It was her father. He and her stepmother were spending the winter in Zurich. Her father was attending a conference. Eve's mother and stepfather were spending the winter in Santa Fe. Neither parent was ever in New York anymore. Eve communicated with them both primarily by telephone.

"How's Switzerland?" She tried to keep the depression out of her tone. She'd tell him another time that Charles César had left.

"Lots of snow here," he said. "Your stepmother has been buying a lot of clothes that don't fit."

Eve laughed.

"What's new, Snoopy?" he asked, using his favorite pet name for her.

"Oh, lots of things. I found something out."

"What?"

"Charlie's Jewish."

There was a silence on the other end of the phone.

"Dad?"

"My goodness," her father said. "Snoop, you say you found out?"

"Well, he converted to Catholicism when he was sixteen so

he doesn't think about it that much and we were talking——"

"Oh, I see," he sounded relieved and worried at the same time. "I always thought he looked like Cardinal Richelieu."

"Me too, Dad."

There was another silence; then her father asked, "Anything else new?"

"No."

She wouldn't tell him about the tattoo. If and when he ever came into town would be time enough.

"Well, that's exciting, Snoop." Her father always looked on the bright side. "Is that okay with you?"

"Of course, Dad."

"Henry Kissinger's here at the conference."

"Nice segue, Dad."

"Okay. I'm just between meetings here and they're announcing lunch. Be good, Snoop. Your stepmother sends love."

"I miss you, Dad."

"Stiff upper snout, Snoop."

And they hung up.

XII

When Eve awoke she was weeping. Her brain felt fuzzy, and a grim decoction of anguish and loss sloshed around under her skin. She opened her eyes, flicked them around the bedroom, and felt the teardrops streaming into her ears. Precognitive sorrow, she called this, that seemed to follow out of dreams she could not recall. Charlie's gone, she muttered. And since she was keeping the tattoo, he would never come back. It's over, she muttered, as if to press this reality upon her emotions.

Eve dragged herself out of bed. She had lost weight and energy, and an empty-shell-longing-for-a-nutmeat feeling threatened to drive her mad. Charlie'd been gone only two weeks. She wondered if she'd survive.

It was Thanksgiving Day, which made it worse. Ordinarily she would have gone to Marcus and Cilla's, but Charlie was staying there so she had declined. Instead, she was dining with her Uncle Jim, who had AIDS.

As she forced herself to get dressed up and put on makeup, she played a game. What were the good things about Charlie being gone? Well, the loft was neat for one thing. Charlie never picked up after himself. He just stepped out of his beautiful clothes and left them in a heap on the floor. It was as if he were creating his own nest, and she couldn't stand it. It offended her sense of order. In truth, his looseness revolted her a little. In the beginning, she used to tease him, Did you have servants in the castle? Or, You must've been demerit king at Catholic school. But then she stopped. He hated her to refer to his past and it brought her no information. Now she understood. He had a Jewish mother who did everything for him, that legendary figure whom she'd learned about from Philip Roth and Woody Allen, the one who spoiled her son for every other woman.

And yet, she thought, as she readied herself to leave, he didn't seem to be that damaged. He seemed to adore her in his own, formal way. It was just the tattoo that had come between them, and then the anger he held about his parents. She hoped that, in time, maybe he would miss her, and he would see that the tattoo—forget it, Eve, she said to herself. It's over, she said to herself. You're keeping the tattoo and he's Jewish and it offends him and he's never coming back. Get him out of your heart, she said to herself. And then, what? Ghetto him out of your heart.

Eve went out of her building and began walking across Greenwich Village. Her destination was the Lily coffee shop where she was to meet her Uncle Jim. The Village was quiet on Thanksgiving Day. Here and there, small clumps of displaced persons, all dressed up, trooped toward tiny apartments where they would huddle together to eat a turkey and simulate family. They were aggressively joyful, and when Eve passed them, she could feel how thrilled they were to be going somewhere for the sole purpose of food and warmth. They were smiling deeply like the Communists on TV who were escaping Communism. It was as if, for one afternoon, they were walking toward freedom.

Aside from the clumps of displaced persons, there was no one about. The Village was overcast and nippy. The decibel level in the streets had dropped from a dull roar to a barely audible dissonance. Eve passed the location where she and Charlie had spent their first date and, inadvertently, she began to grieve. The Romanian restaurant where he had taken her had long ago closed. Two Italian bistros, a yuppie diner, and a health-food boutique had occupied the place in the years intervening, but it made no difference. Eve always thought of that night when she passed it, every time she passed it, doing laundry, running to the subway, out of the corner of her mind. Eve could never quite believe how romantic she was. There was this steel-trap mind and then this gooey depth of romance, like she was encased in armor that was oiled with honey.

Eve turned a corner and entered an area of the Village that had been devastated by AIDS. The cluster of streets, once the jaunty haunt of drag queens and box-office managers, decorators and the decorated, fey boys in cowboy gear and leather draped with chains, was deserted now. The bath shop, the leather G-string shop, the antique clothing shop with pumps size ten and up, the pornographic bakery were gone, all gone with the wind that carried the virus.

Once, on Bleecker Street, Eve had come across a man in a nurse's costume doing a drag show. He stood in the middle of traffic, lip-syncing the score to *Bye Bye Birdie,* which was blaring from speakers set up in the windows of his apartment. He was very funny, tall and gawky in his nurse's shoes and starched uniform and perky cap, and he threw himself into the performance, swooning over the hoods of taxis and limos during the love songs. When, finally, he was forced onto the sidewalk by a beet-red rookie cop whom he taunted sexily and shamelessly, a gathered crowd applauded wildly. He made the deep curtsy of a prima ballerina and exited into his building.

Eve had always wondered what had made him do it. Why that day, why the nurse's costume, why *Bye Bye Birdie?* And why in the middle of traffic, which was dangerous. She had fantasized a midwestern childhood for him that was phobic and terrifying: a father who would slit his throat if his son's predilections were known; a mother far too empathetic for her son's own good or anyone else's. A local clergyman, no, doctor, with a taste for teen boys, and around everything, silence, that silence that envelops the aberrational, protecting it from censure, but hiding it in hell. But perhaps it wasn't that way at all.

The AIDS rights activists called AIDS a holocaust, but that was inaccurate. The holocaust was the holocaust. The Nazis hunted down and exterminated gays because they were gay. AIDS was a cataclysm, a disaster, a virus that was in the right place at the right time and became a superstar. The activists had it wrong: AIDS was not personal. The holocaust was personal.

Eve had a dear friend, Henry, who had died so early that when he called her and told her he had AIDS, she had never heard of it.

"I'm dying," Henry had said.

"What do you mean you're dying?"

"I have AIDS."

"What is that—a form of leukemia?" She named something a young man could die of.

"No," he replied bitterly. "It's the gay plague."

Eve never believed Henry was going to die. Cancer, she kept thinking, remission, but the months that followed that conversation were something biblical.

She remembered scenes as she crossed the Village, passing places she and Henry had passed. Henry, before, coming out of a dressing cubicle, head to toe in black leather with cowboy boots and hat. "Do I look macho?" he asked. Before, at dinner. He looked angelic. His skin was almost transparent, parchment thin. He laughed at her joke, after which he laid his head on the table, hollow-eyed and exhausted and utterly scared. Henry, after, at his house. "Look at this. Watch this," he said. And he tried to touch his finger to his nose, missing completely, touching his cheek. Henry, after, in the hospital, covered with rashes, swollen, his brain cut up and restapled together. "I'm moving to the deco wing of the hospital. I hate it here." He managed to raise himself and got on the phone, lapsing into a coma between each call, until it was done.

When he got the deco room and the view of the river, he started to die. "Just hold my hand, Evie," he said, and they no longer spoke. Eve held his hand, day after day, while the locusts set upon his body and ate it clean. Toward the end, he sat up one day and said lucidly, "The cat gave me a brain tumor. Because of the fucking cat, I'm going to die."

And then he did.

Several weeks later, she traveled to Los Angeles. One of the people she saw there was her Uncle Jim. She made an appointment with him specially because he was gay and so precious to her. They sat in the garden of his house on Orange Grove, and she told him everything she knew about AIDS.

"You've got to be careful," she kept saying. "It's no joke. You've got to be really careful."

One night about a year and a half later, at two in the morning, her phone cried out in the night and it was her Uncle Jim. He was sobbing.

She sat bolt upright in the dark. She knew before he told her.

"I'm sick," he said, that terrible phrase that had come to mean "in two years I'll be dead."

She burst into tears and then a speechlessness came on her, and a vision: Henry covered with welts, one side of his head shaved and stapled together.

"I love you, Uncle Jim," she managed.

"Oh, Eve,"

They listened to each other cry.

"Where are you?" she asked.

"In a bar in Chicago."

She could hear the clink of glasses and laughter in the background. She pictured his lanky, funny figure hunched on a bar stool, weeping.

"What are you doing there?"

"I'm driving back to New York."

He mentioned this possibility in L.A. He was fed up with his career there as a comic actor. "If I have to play another decorator or wacky next-door neighbor, I think I'll go mad," he had said.

"When will you get here?" she asked.

"In a week."

"Will you be seeing your mother?"

"Yes, but I won't tell her. She's eighty. Why does she have to know?"

"No, no reason. . . . Uncle Jim?"

"Yes, Eve?"

There was a long silence then.

The afternoon on Orange Grove, Eve had told Jim everything that could happen to him in grisly detail. She thought she was protecting him. It never occurred to her that it might already be too late.

Eve remembered hanging up the phone that night and screaming. The man in bed next to her, a sexual friend, had the good sense to immediately put his arms around her and hold her close while her anguish spewed out into the dark.

She had known Jim since she was six years old. When Eve's parents had divorced, her mother had remarried, moved to the City, and lived next door to him. Eve was living with her grandparents.

Since Jim was gay and had no children, he pronounced himself her honorary uncle. And when she visited her mother on weekends, she would wander into his apartment and stare at the salamander he kept in a fish tank. Those were tragic days for Eve, alleviated only by Jim's empathy and fun.

He was then a young actor in his twenties, a brilliant graduate of the Art Institute of Chicago, and was often home during the day. One weekend, when it rained and stormed and her mother's new baby was demanding her attention, Jim had drawn and painted for Eve an entire family of Victorian paper dolls. Their costumes were in perfect period: hats with plumes, corsets, high boots, lovely and funny, works of art. Or then there was the egg hunt at Easter. Her mother wrote poems as clues while Jim had dyed the eggs and painted them with edible watercolor. She would never forget finding each one. They were extraordinary, in violet hues, parodies of Fabergé.

But what she remembered most of all was how funny and graceful a person he was. About five-foot-nine like Charlie, but spindly, furtive, and mischievous, an Irish intellectual with an incisive but lyrical humor that was always erudite.

"Let's play Lady Murasaki, Eve," he would cry, fluttering his long fingers at the six-year-old. And he would sit down and strum the koto while Eve played at making tea. His command of the Japanese lyre was magical, a by-product of his Asian art studies at the university.

In that place of his, so long ago, the rain thundering at the window, bathed in the warm light of potential, lulled by the lyricism of the porcelain-faced ancients, Eve had learned something about happiness and more about love. And the thought of what awaited this man on the rack of pain and terror to which fate had now tied him was almost impossible for her to bear.

Jim was already in the booth when Eve entered the Lily. She bent down to give him a kiss on the cheek and he winced imperceptibly. He was afraid to be touched and also afraid he was contagious, but it went beyond that. He was no longer in bodily contact with the world. It could be read in his posture: I don't touch people anymore, his musculature shouted, and they don't touch me.

Jim had Kaposi's sarcoma. As Eve sat down, she smiled at him, checking his face to see if any lesions were visible. No. He looked fine. He appeared to be the same weight. She breathed a sigh of relief. It was Thanksgiving. He was in a cheery mood. It was family time. Death could wait out in the alley until the thanks had been given.

"Did you see this review by Frank Rich?"

He waved the previous day's newspaper at her.

"No. Of what?"

"The Andrei Serban thing at Lincoln Center."

"Yes?"

" 'Unencumbered by words,' it says, 'the actors, unencumbered by words'—what in God's name can he be thinking of?"

"A lot easier to review, I guess," Eve said, and they both rolled their eyes in mock despair.

The Lily coffee shop was full on the holiday, mostly with gay men and elderly people and two very young punk couples. For the occasion, the Greeks had festooned the place with strings of dime-store paper turkeys, and plastic ears of corn and squash. A real pumpkin sat by the cash register, a proud symbol of their understanding of the new world, proof that the ways of the Pilgrim fathers had not escaped them. And the menu featured turkey with trimmings alongside the usual spanakopita and stuffed grape leaves.

"They're very excited about Thanksgiving here," Eve said smiling. "I'm glad we came here instead of going someplace fancy. It's exactly what I need."

"Poor Eve," said her Uncle Jim.

He touched her hand ever so lightly, almost not touching it, careful not to contaminate her.

"I always thought you chose Charlie because he was like me," he said. "Are you terribly sad?"

"Yes, and I did," Eve said, and the weight of the truth made her droop. "But it's all right. It's all right."

"What happened, dear? You seemed to love each other."

Eve was going to tell him about the tattoo, but she decided against it. In due time he would notice and then she would tell him his tale.

"We do. That never stopped anyone from committing crime, did it?"

"No," he replied. "In a way I'm thrilled to be out of all that. In a way it's a great relief."

Eve wondered if this were really true. She thought of the loneliness he must feel, of the isolation. She thought not.

"How are you?" she asked in such a way that he knew she meant AIDS.

"All right," he said, sweeping all emotion out of his being, going clinical. "I had the lesions on my face removed with acid this week. It works quite well."

She peered at him, obviously scanning his face now.

"It looks good," she agreed.

"My white blood cells are behaving themselves, but my on-cologist says I'm not on AZT."

"How does *he* know?" Eve asked petulantly.

Eve silently cursed doctors. Jim was part of an experimental program that didn't tell him whether he was getting the drug or a placebo. They didn't tell him so his hopes wouldn't be dashed.

"He says my blood tests would be more erratic or something. He says he knows."

Eve tried to speak, but her voice wouldn't come. She wrestled with herself and finally got out,

"They say AZT is pretty virulent. They say it doesn't really . . ."

"No," he agreed, nodding to himself. "Eve, I want to ask you something."

The tone of his voice was so intimate that Eve felt as if around their table, the lights had lowered, and a spotlight had come up on his face.

"Yes, Uncle Jim."

"If I can't get the materials from my Italian doctor friend, will you go to Mexico and get me what I need to commit suicide?"

Eve stopped moving. She had to think hard before answering this question. This question was the newfangled thing that the AIDS epidemic had brought them, a contact with mass death in life that, once the Vietnam War was over, they thought they would never have again. These strange core moments of necrotic complexity threatened to drain the last of her youth right away.

Like that day in the bank, when she ran into her ex-agent, a bitchy, campy queen, age forty-one, and she innocently, offhandedly, making-conversationally asked, "Where have you been? I haven't seen you around."

"Oh, you don't know," he said with concern for her. "I'm sick."

And there she was, standing disgruntled in the line for the teller, hard by bad art, under neon light, confronting the living death of a friend she had known for twenty years. To fill the space left by her shock, he made a joke. "They're giving me mood elevators because I'm depressed because I'm dying of AIDS."

She laughed and then she said, "I'm so sorry."

87

The most inadequate phrase on the planet.

What had happened, she asked herself, that these terrifying moments of seriousness were played out in these mundane settings, the bank, the coffee shop? Would she go down to Mexico to purchase suicide materials for her dear uncle. Would she? She visualized the trip down to Nogales, alone in the car, her heart thumping. If you assist in this manner, even if you, as she did, agreed that suicide was okay in such a Jobian case, well, not okay, but understandable, did that make you liable? Would that fuck you up with God? Could she stand up and face God and say, "Yes, I thought it was wrong for him to die in anguish. Right to take his own life. Yes. I helped. I'm proud of it."

She didn't want her Uncle Jim to take his own life. She did not think it would come to that. If she had AIDS, would she? Yes, probably.

"I don't know. I think so," she replied honestly. "If it came to it. If there was no other way. So you would have the option."

"Thank you," he said meaning it more than she had ever heard it said.

She saw herself entering one of those dinky *farmacias* on the Mexican side of Nogales where Americans swarmed to buy codeina-aspirina and Retin-A. "Five bottles of Seconal *por favor.*"

Sometimes Eve found life so grim, she dreamed of becoming an old whore, of drinking and fucking her life away in total irresponsibility. Totally careless, totally gone and wasted, wallowing in the faux freedom of the lost.

Her Uncle Jim was Catholic, so she asked him now, "Uncle Jim, how do you really feel about suicide? Do you think you will have to do time? I've had an abortion. I expect to do some time. I'm prepared to do some time."

"No," he said quietly. "No, under the circumstances, I believe God will be merciful."

They looked at each other for a few moments, and then fell back into coffee-shop mode. AIDS was gone, the specter of Henry with the staples in his head, Eve's creeping figure on a dusty Nogales side street.

88

"What do you think about Eastern Europe?" Eve asked.

"Well, I suppose we'll have to put up with a lot of Polish and Czech actors longing to do Clifford Odets," Uncle Jim replied.

"What about Germany?"

"The Wall was wonderful. Of course they'll want to reunify now."

The waiter brought the food and their drinks. Jim interrupted himself to toast Eve with his decaf. "Happy Thanksgiving, Evie."

"Happy Thanksgiving, Uncle Jim."

She glanced at him lovingly and her emotion caused them both to lower their eyes. They drank.

"Reunify," Eve asked. "You think?"

"Of course, a comeback. East and West Germany, together, again."

He shook himself. "A dreadful thought."

"You think after all this time there's still a problem?" Eve asked.

"I certainly do, dear."

"Why?"

"Because by nature they're cold and bestial. Beautiful lovers, though."

He smiled, remembering some German godlet he had ravished on a long-ago trip to Greece. "Helmut," he murmured, "the loveliest honey skin I have ever seen."

By nature, she thought to herself. Really? By nature? She reached for her glass and her sleeve fell down her arm and Jim spied the tattoo.

"What is that, Eve?" he asked, pinning her up against the booth with his look.

"It's the I.D. number of an Auschwitz victim," she replied.

"An Auschwitz victim?" he repeated.

He took hold of her forearm and inspected the tattoo.

"Five-oh-oh-one-two-three. What does that mean? The five hundred thousandth one hundred and twenty-third prisoner of the Reich?"

"I don't know. Her name was Eva Marks. She was a German Red Cross nurse."

They stared at each other across the table and then her Uncle Jim leaned back. "Why are you wearing that?" he asked.

"I'm wearing it in remembrance," she replied. "Would you like to hear about her?"

"Tell me," he said.

"Okay," she replied. "Eva Marks was a German Red Cross nurse. In 1942, she was assigned to the Bahnhof Station in Berlin. Along with five other nurses, she was directed to dispense drinking water to wounded troops arriving from the eastern front."

The Bahnhof was a madhouse in that period, Eve went on. Trains were running twenty hours late, if at all. Soldiers were traveling from one area of the Reich to another. Civilians, fleeing the Allied bombings, thronged the platforms, laden with as many of their belongings as they could carry. Babies were wailing. Dogs were barking. But there was a general air of making-do and bustle that was curiously festive.

Eva set up her water buckets at one end of her assigned platform. She organized her tin cups and sat down on a stool awaiting the trains. She was glad to be in the station. She had been working in makeshift field hospitals in the badly bombed areas of the city, tending the wounds of women and children. The duty had been frightening and sad.

For weeks she had been inhaling plaster dust and particles of metal and debris, which had given her a persistent cough. Her skin was broken out from dirt and tension. The station would be a lark after that. Eva needed a lark. She was almost thirty-six years old. Germany had been at war since she was thirty-two. She was losing her good years to chaos.

Eva served two troop trains that afternoon, fetching and dispensing water, dripping drops of liquid into the mouths of dying boys, laughing for the living wounded, smiling for the unhurt. There was one more troop train to come, scheduled for eleven that evening. It was only 8 p.m., three hours to wait, and

Eva was unusually tired. Praying she wasn't pregnant, she settled on her stool, closed her eyes, and fell asleep.

She was jolted awake by a train arriving on the opposite platform, on the track going east. It wasn't just the whistles, screeches, and thunder that woke her, but a groundswell of human moaning that sucked her from her slumber and hurled her into consciousness.

She jerked up and saw pulling in a long train of cattle cars with what looked like children's arms and hands extending through the air vents near the bottom of the doors.

She stood up, almost involuntarily, out of a knee-jerk sense of duty, confused, not sure she was seeing what she was seeing, not sure what to do, when about fifty SS men appeared, flanked by about a hundred foreign POWs. The SS ran the dogs and the POWs down the platform and stationed three men at the door of every car. At the shrill sound of a whistle, the train halted, and the men unlocked and slid open the doors and shouted at those inside to throw out their dead.

Eva was dumbstruck. Inside the cars, men, women, and children, civilians by the look of them, were mashed together, standing upright. Some, who were already dead, fell out the doors like pick-up sticks onto the platform. Others, desperate to breathe fresh air, dropped to their knees in the spaces now free and inhaled for their lives.

They looked terrible, exhausted, filthy. Mortification darkened their eyes. But in ludicrous contrast to their dreadful plight, they were all dressed up: fur coats, hats with feathers, silk stockings, polished leather shoes, as if they thought they were going to a luncheon and been arrested instead.

Eve saw now that it had been children's arms and hands pushing through the vents. Little children were shoving to the front of the cars, toward the open doors, trying to get out, trying to climb down. Little ones, two and three years old just like hers. The POWs pushed them back into the cars with long sticks.

"Water!"

The adults in the cars were imploring her and the other nurses on the platform.

"Water!"

"Who are they?" Eva asked the SS man nearest her.

"Jews," he snapped. "Stay away!"

So this is what happened to them, she thought. This was one of the transports she'd heard about. She surveyed the train. Some cars had the Red Cross insignia painted on them. There's something wrong with that, she thought. Some babies had been hurt. They were screaming in agony. This can't be sanctioned by the Red Cross, she thought. I'm going to see about this.

She gestured down the platform at the other nurses and asked them with her hands: Shall we give water? The others shrugged and then nodded okay. But Eva Marks was the only one who moved. She picked up her bucket and carried it past the SS man to the cattle car's open door.

It happened so quickly that it was a long time before she realized what hit her. But the other nurses saw clearly. It was the SS man's foot. He came right up behind her to the edge of the platform where she was doling out water, and he kicked her in the small of the back, propelling her inside the car. Then he ordered the door slammed shut. She scrambled hysterically, pounding on the door until the train left the station, but the other nurses dared not come to her aid. The Red Cross protested. Attempts were made to free her. But the papers got lost in the bureaucracy of the camp, and so did Eva. She was gassed by mistake at Auschwitz six months later.

Eve and her Uncle Jim sat in silence for a while and then Eve said again, "I'm wearing her number in remembrance."

Jim nodded.

"That's why Charlie left me," she said, "because I had this number tattooed on my arm. He can't understand. Can you, Jim?"

XIII

The bouncer at the door of the rock club was a huge, dumb bodybuilder. His shoulders, Eve thought, look like two challah breads joined at his neck.

"Marie Hawkins. Day Job," Eve said to him.

The name of the A&R person. The name of the band. Eve spoke these passwords with more authority than she felt. Going to see Marie's bands had taught her that the more authority you had in your voice, the more you got in the rock world, no matter who you were or what you were up to. Unless you got bitchy. If you got bitchy, a guy like the bouncer would strangle with stifled rage. You would remind him of his mother on a bad day. He wouldn't let you in if his job were at stake. That's how much power mothers had. If only they could keep it in mind.

Eve passed under the velvet rope and into the rock club called Kawabunga, or "how ya doin'" in sixties surfer slang. It was the first time she and Eva had been out clubbing together.

Now that Charles César was gone, Eve had begun to talk to Eva in her mind. Their relationship had progressed from remembrance to cohabitation, from the past to the present. People, Eve thought, would think her mad if they knew. But they'd be wrong. It was keeping her sane. Eve had planned no tales for the evening. The girls were off duty. They were out to have some fun.

Eve took a stroll around the main room, which was decorated in sixties surfing motif. This was an ethic that seemed to be lost on the twenty-year-old New Yorkers who jammed the place. Eve watched them as they peered at the old surfboards on the wall with scientific interest. She eavesdropped as they pointed at the coconut-shell drink glasses behind the bar and wondered about their function. A huge, plaster wave curl, a replica of the one on the old TV show "Hawaii Five-O," rolled out of the wall and became a bar. Eve hung at it for a time, observing the young crowd as they examined the black-light posters pinned up over every table. To them, Eve thought, Jimi Hendrix was an old guy. Then she explained to Eva who he was.

Eve found Marie sitting with her band over in a dark corner by the stage.

"Hi," Marie said. "Don't you love this place? Isn't it funny?"

"I feel compelled to hang ten," Eve replied.

The band laughed and Eve smiled playfully at the very young men. Not bad, eh, Eva? she thought. Marie introduced each member and Eve sat down.

"You'll see when the next band comes on the whole crowd will change. The next band's a New York band. See that guy?"

Marie was pointing to a techie type, aged about forty-two with long, grizzled hippie hair, who was messing with a projector near the stage.

"That guy used to be part of the Joshua Light Show. He's got the original, what do you call them, gels, slides."

"Really?" Eve said. "What a funny place."

The bass player for the band moved his chair, sat down opposite Eve, and began to talk to her, making silly little jokes. He was about twenty-five with brown curly hair and an angelic face. He was tall and wearing a black coat with the collar turned up as young men often do to look cool. Eve played with him for a while and then turned back to Marie.

"I haven't spoken to Charlie," Eve muttered glumly.

"He's a fool," said Marie loyally.

"Maybe," said Eve.

"Who's Charlie?" the bass player interrupted. "Not your boyfriend, I hope?"

Eve laughed. "Not anymore. We're separated." She glanced at Marie.

"I haven't said that out loud before."

"How are you, Evie?" Marie asked.

"Awful," Eve replied. "If I didn't have Eva,"—she glanced down at the tattoo, which was covered by a sleeve—"I'd be so lonely."

Marie sighed. Then she perked up and whispered in Eve's ear. "He likes you."

She was referring to the young bass player.

"I'm a hundred years older than him, for God's sake," Eve whispered back.

"He doesn't seem to notice," Marie replied. "Look, I told you."

As she'd predicted, the twenty-year-old crowd was leaving the club and a new, hard-looking, thirtyish throng of biker types and bottle-blondes in ragged black was filtering in.

"You know, I think they'd love surfing in Eastern Europe," Eve said. "We should ship the contents of this club over to them as a present. Shoot de curl. Follow dat vave." She simulated a Slavic accent for Eva's benefit.

Marie didn't answer. Her attention was elsewhere. Music business people were arriving.

A young woman in record publishing came in coked to the gills and red-eyed but on the case.

"Hi. Hi." She greeted everyone by nodding her head, up and down, up and down, constantly. "Fucking cold out there. Who's here?" She swiveled her head around the room. "Kaufmann. That's good. That's good."

Marie nodded back. She was the kind of girl that mirrored your behavior when she felt awkward. It usually worked. If one was on coke, it worked really well.

"I'm going to the bathroom," the young woman said. She eyed the bass player who had been talking to Eve and gave him a steamy look. Then she trotted away.

"Hi, Arthur. God, you look healthy."

Marie was turning on the charm. It was Arthur Kaufmann, president of a hot, small record company. He had stopped doing drugs and drinking about four months earlier. He looked awful and he was in a foul mood.

"For what it's fucking worth," he snarled.

He bent down and pecked Marie on the cheek. With him was a huge, beefy kid whose job was to keep dealers and drinks away from Arthur. It was said that the kid slept in Arthur's bedroom at night, watched as Arthur and his wife had sex, maybe even joined in. The kid never left Arthur's side except to run to the bar for the chain of Diet Cokes that Arthur consumed throughout the evening.

The New York band came onto the bandstand now, and the biker crowd settled in. The band members wore torn black clothing, and, through the holes, black tattoos could be seen on their arms and chests. The lead singer, who was bone thin with dyed black hair, had an earring tattooed on his earlobe.

Look, Eva! Eve stood up and moved closer to the bandstand. Tattoos! Black ones like yours, only abstract, like clan designations from Africa or the South Pacific.

The band kicked off, and a few minutes into the first song, the Joshua Light guy began to do his stuff. Over the metallic clanging of the guitars, playing with the rhythm, he popped a black-and-white checkboard slide onto the screen behind the band, which made the audience gasp.

Eva, look!

"What the fuck is that?" a biker guy in front of them asked his friend.

"Op art," the friend replied. "Remember op art?"

The psychedelics popped on now, swirly, patterns within patterns, mostly black and white but also butter yellows and turquoise blues. The lead guitarist stepped into them and they undulated across his body in perfect time to his music. Look, Eva, look. The audience oohed and aahed like innocents.

"This is a real light show." The coked-out publishing girl's voice rose above the din. "This is fucking amazing."

Over there! Eve gasped. Eva, over there! Eve was referring to the bikers in front of her who, she had just noticed, were covered in tattoos. Peeping out from under their shirtsleeves, inching up their necks, lovely muted Renaissance colors created a fairy tale. A fragile princess, Eva, the head of a snow-white swan. A goblin's foot, and—

One of the biker guys turned his head and caught her looking. Eve thought he would be angry, like Big Dan, with that biker's contempt, so violent and scary, but no, he bent right down and rolled up his pants legs and then his shirtsleeves.

As the guitars mourned soulfully, he exhibited his tattoos for them. He pulled up the shirt of his biker friend and displayed the man's back. Eva, look! The ceiling of the Sistine Chapel. A scene from *A Midsummer-Night's Dream*. The two biker guys were beaming. They grinned through op art light masks.

The band was reaching the crescendo. The slide flipped to a yin-and-yang symbol that slid around like an amoeba. The crowd was cheering. The biker guys did one more turn for them, pumping up their biceps so breasts would quiver and Adam's finger touched Eve. Eva, show them yours, Eve said, and she pointed to her forearm and rolled up her sleeve.

The bikers looked. Their smiles faded. They didn't understand. They smiled politely. Never mind, Eva, what do they know? What do we care?

Eve felt two hands clasp her shoulders. She looked up and saw the young bass player had come up behind her. He bent down and whispered in her ear. "Can I come home with you tonight?"

The yin-and-yang pattern was liquid on his face. Desire was dripping out of his eyes. He really wanted her.

I'm a hundred years older than him, Eva. What do you think? Go for it, Eva replied.

XIV

The young bass player cocked his head and smiled.

"Hi," he said.

"Hi," replied Eve, looking over his naked torso with a satisfied purr.

"Hey, what's this?" he asked, running his long fingers over the tattoo.

"Oh," Eve said, surprised, "oh."

She paused, then said, "It's a prisoner I.D. number from a Nazi concentration camp."

"Oh," he said, examining it, "were you in a camp?"

"What?" she asked.

"Were you in a Nazi camp?" he asked again.

Eve looked at him sharply. She had told him she was thirty-five. He was looking back at her, concerned, empathetic, sincere. Could it be he didn't know that World War II ended in 1945?

"Yes," she ventured. "Yes. I was at Auschwitz."

He saw no contradiction there. He just felt rotten about it.

"Wow," he said. "The Nazis were really mean, weren't they?"

"Yes," she replied. "Really mean."

"How old were you?" he asked.

She replied carefully.

"Eighteen."

"Boy"—he shook his head sadly—"when I was eighteen, I

was playing in a garage band and smoking dope in the Dairy Queen parking lot. I feel like a jerk."

"No."

She took his hand.

"Don't feel like a jerk. Feel lucky. Feel how lucky you are."

"How come you went there?" he asked uncertainly, not sure it was all right to do so.

She smiled to reassure him.

"I'm Jewish," she said.

"Really?"

He was surprised.

"You don't look Jewish. I wouldn't have known that."

"Well, that's the reason I was sent there, but it's not the reason I was arrested. I was arrested for a traffic violation. I got a speeding ticket."

"You're kidding me, now." He pushed her shoulder.

"No," she said soberly. "No, I'm not. I remember it very well. It was June fifteenth of the year I turned eighteen that the Nazis arrested fifteen hundred Jewish citizens with police records, including those convicted of traffic violations. I was one of those."

"I want to hear," he said, snuggling up to her.

"Okay," she replied. "It was a lovely summer's day. I remember that because I wanted badly to go out but my sister was in trouble with our parents. The sun was shining through the open windows. The birds were twittering and my sister was sitting on this red velvet chair we had, a big overstuffed one with tassels for a skirt. My mother was hysterical. My father was furious."

My father was home all the time now, she said. He had been fired from the newspaper, about five years before, after the Nazis enacted the Law of Editors, which barred all Jewish editors from editorial work. In that time, he had had one menial job after another, all of which he eventually lost, and on this day I'm telling you about, he was unemployed.

The problem was this: my parents had found out that my 99

sister, who was twenty, was dating an Aryan. Well, actually, it was just Friedrich, her high-school boyfriend whom she'd dated since she was sixteen, but they'd demanded she break off with him three years earlier, and she hadn't done it and she'd lied to them.

See, three years before, the Nazis had passed these laws about the position of Jews in Germany called the Nuremburg Laws. And one of these laws, the Law for the Protection of German Blood and German Honor, made sex and marriage between Jews and non-Jews illegal.

The young bass player shifted nervously. Eve went on.

Well, that's how ugly it was, you know. Anyway, that's the law that got my sister. She flipped out. She and Friedrich were wild about each other. They had their whole life planned.

For myself, I couldn't see Friedrich. He was tall and emaciated with carrot-colored hair and no eyelashes, and no color in his skin at all. But there's no accounting for taste, and my sister decided to risk everything to go on seeing him. Three years went by and she managed to get away with it. My parents were so distraught over the state of our Jewish lives, they failed to notice what she was doing.

Things were getting worse and worse. We used to take drives with my father on Sundays but we had to stop that. At the entrance to each village we passed through, signs were now posted that read, JEWS NOT WANTED HERE, and it was really scary. Then we heard that Reinhard Heydrich, the head of the Gestapo, had ordered "protective custody" for any "defilers of the race." This meant torture, prison, or concentration camp, automatically for any Jew who slept with a non-Jew and vice versa. I talked to my sister about this but she refused to listen. She was now risking not only her life and Friedrich's, but the lives of both our families by spooning with this weedy boy, but she wouldn't stop.

The day the Gestapo came to arrest me was the day my parents found out about my sister. Friedrich's mother had caught them together in the basement below Friedrich's father's butcher shop. She phoned my mother hysterical and told her. It was ironic, really, because all afternoon my parents were out of their minds about it.

"What are you doing? How can you keep going with one of them?" my mother was screaming.

"You'll get us all arrested, you fool, and for what?" my father was bellowing.

"What's wrong with you?" my mother.

"You have disgraced and endangered us!" my father.

"You're a tramp and a heathen!" my mother over the top.

"Surely you can find a Jewish man to love!" my father, pointedly.

My sister was crying but defiant.

"I have false papers I carry when I'm with him. You'll never be implicated. No one will know you're my family," she cried.

"Wunderbar," my father muttered.

My mother sobbed.

"You're all so afraid, it disgusts me!" My sister was screaming now. "I hate it! I hate it!"

This was the moment the Gestapo chose to pound on the door. My sister shut up. My mother and father looked at her with sheer hatred in their eyes. I, who had been observing the proceedings and was relatively calm, went to the door and answered it.

"Eva Flick," the Gestapo man said sharply.

I was shocked.

"Yes," I said, "I am she."

"Come with us," he snapped. "You're under arrest."

I was so stunned that I actually questioned the Gestapo. "What have I done?" I asked.

Taken by surprise, he answered spontaneously, "You have a police record. We're arresting all Jews with police records."

Police record? I was totally perplexed.

"The speeding ticket," my mother said, and she and my father threw up their hands in despair.

It was just a few months ago that I had been sitting in the same red velvet chair surrounded by the same screaming parents, screaming over my speeding ticket.

"We mustn't give them anything to hang on to," my father had roared.

"They don't need anything, for God's sake, we've learned that," I shouted back.

I was right but I wasn't right. The Nazis liked their bureaucratic cloak. They liked to keep up appearances.

I remember saying to the Gestapo man as we left the apartment, "It was only five miles above the speed limit."

I was sent to Dachau and then, after several years, to Auschwitz. My parents did not survive but my sister did. She went into hiding, aided by Friedrich. She spent four years in that basement of his father's shop.

"Wow," the young man said. "Come 'ere."

And he put his arms around Eve and began to caress her.

It turns him on, Eve thought. It turns on a man I don't love and turns off a man I do love. Charlie's right: you mess with this Nazi stuff, you get all fucked up.

XV

Charles César opened the door to Cilla and Marcus's brownstone. It was Christmas Eve and Cilla and Marcus and Nora had
gone off to a Christmas pageant at Nora's church school. Charlie
looked odd to Eve, standing there proprietarily on the threshold
of this foreign house, opening the door for her, letting her in,
directing her up the stairs to the living room. He was beginning
to reassume his bachelorisms, to appear jaunty and uncon-
nected. It made her sad.

"'Ow are you?" Charlie asked when they were finally seated
and he had given her a drink.

"Lousy," Eve replied and laughed ruefully. "How are you?"

"I don' know," he said glumly. "Ah'm working very hard and
trying to finish my film. It's amusing living here."

"I bet. Nice having little Nora around, and Cilla and Marcus
must be funny?"

"Yes, that's it," he replied.

Eve wondered if he had slept with someone else, too. It was
possible. Perhaps that jaunty walk indicated something, though
Eve had reached the age when sexual infidelity was such a small
thing compared to the other infidelities that could be perpetrated in the name of love. Like her tattoo. Like his disgust
with it.

"What do you think about reunification?" Eve wanted to take

them away from the personal. It was Christmas Eve, a sappy time. Things could get out of hand.

"Ours or the Germans'?" Charlie asked.

Eve laughed.

"First the Germans', " Eve said.

"You know I don' trust their nationalism and I never will." Charlie's voice was hard. "And neither does the rest of Europe," he added.

"What about these Romanians?" Eve missed talking with Charlie. She was enjoying this. "It really is the land of Vlad the Impaler, is it not?"

"Unbelievable ferocity," he said.

"Maybe they should close Eastern Europe back up. It's pretty weird in there. Pandora's box. When I used to hear the term 'Baltic States,' I pictured blue seas and palm trees. I was clearly off the track."

"Yes, you were. It never fails to amaze me how little history Americans know. It's so strange to me to live in a world and know so little about it and how it evolved."

"Yeah. This is why they forced me to read *Bartleby the Scrivener,* by Melville, when I was in grammar school. As I recall, all he ever says is 'Nothing. I know nothing. I prefer not.' It was like swallowing cardboard. I hated it, but it's definitely American. On the other hand we got away with knowing nothing for a fair amount of time before getting caught out. Who knew the world was going to change overnight and require some adult thought?"

"Ah'm counting on the Soviets now to keep some perspective with this German thing. They won't go all gooey like the West."

"Yes, well, they've got their own problems. I always said, 'Any country that has to stand on line for lettuce is no threat to us,' but the Joint Chiefs refused to listen to me."

Charlie laughed at this, then smiled at her and suddenly they felt the intimacy they possessed together quicken and come to life. Tears came to their eyes at the same time. Eve got up and went to survey the Christmas tree.

"Did you make decorations with Nora?" she asked. She was trying to get calm, grasping for nonchalant.

"Yes, I did. It was a lot of fun. I made the rabbi there." He pointed to a little black figure complete with hat and payess made out of origami paper, with a tiny round paper head.

Eve looked closely at it. "It looks like it's been chewed," she said.

"Yes. It was the only one the cat got." Charles César shrugged helplessly. "It's an old story."

She turned and faced him.

"What's it like to be Jewish?" she asked.

"For me, it's a nightmare. You are always embracing it or denying it. And then you are damned if you do and damned if you don't."

"Why did you invite me here?"

Eve went to the fireplace and warmed herself by the fire. In true English fashion, Cilla kept the apartment cold, at fifty-five degrees. Nora never wore a sweater outside in the fall. Nora was never cold.

"Eve."

Charles César's voice cracked when he spoke. He laughed and cleared his throat.

"Eve?"

She looked at him expectantly.

"My parents were catchers," he said and sighed.

"Your parents were catchers?" She repeated this to make sure she had it right.

"Yes."

"Oh God. Oh no." She rushed over to him and put her hands on his shoulders. He was stiff as a rod.

"I'm sorry," she said, the most inadequate phrase on the planet.

He nodded.

The enormity of what she'd done in getting the tattoo overwhelmed her and she repeated, "I'm so sorry."

Charlie looked at her, resigned and bitter. He said nothing.

"Do you know the details?" she asked, finally.

"No," he managed, "not really. Just that they worked for the Gestapo during the war. Just that they were instrumental in the arrests of women and children. Just that they went into hiding in 'forty-four and survived. Just that they were——"

He gestured helplessly with his small hands. He was at a loss to find the worst word.

"Catchers," she said it for him and glanced down at her tattoo. She found herself backing away from him suddenly. She was afraid for Eva. She lighted on an armchair in order to think. She saw tears well up in his eyes.

"I love you," she said. "I truly do."

He closed his eyes and nodded. The tears fell down his cheeks. She sought to give comfort.

"Totalitarianism," she murmured. "Eventually everyone gets caught in the net, even those who think they're safe."

"My parents survived." He hissed this.

"Yes, but they lost you," she said softly.

"Please get it removed. I'm asking you for the last time."

"Help me," she said. "It could be an expiation for you. Maybe Eva was someone they hurt."

"I thought about that when I got the photograph. But it was fantasy."

He made a disgusted sound.

"The tattoo isn't fantasy," she said. "It's a woman's number, a woman who was arrested and corralled."

"A woman you are saving," he said derisively.

"Whose memory I am preserving and honoring for the duration of my life. Think of it like this. It could help you."

"I don't want to think of it at all," he replied.

"I understand that now," said Eve, and they fell silent.

"I miss you," Charles César said after a time.

"I miss you, too, more than you can imagine."

"But?"

"But, if you ask me to choose between your guilt and Eva's

life——"

Clomping was heard on the stairs, then a key in the lock, and Nora rushed into the room followed by Cilla and Marcus. Nora's cheeks were rose red and an expression of joy haloed off her little face.

"Tomorrow is Jesus' birthday. Did you know that?"

"Yes. How old is he, Nora?" asked Eve, distracted.

Nora looked to her mother for the answer. Cilla snorted. "Around one thousand nine-hundred and ninety, dear."

"He's old." Nora was surprised. "He looked like a baby."

"Jesus is in heaven, darling, therefore, strictly speaking, he doesn't have an age." Marcus sniffed. "Everyone got drinks?"

"We saw donkeys and lambs!" Nora boomed with enthusiasm. "Jesus was born with animals around his mother. In a barn. I wish that happened to me!"

"Me, too, dear," said Cilla and everyone laughed. "It is sweet the way they have the crêche with these live baby animals. The children love—Oh, dear! What's happened to your rabbi?"

Cilla addressed this to Charles César. She had approached the tree and noticed the mutilated ornament.

"The cat got it," Charlie said sadly.

Cilla turned to Eve and Charlie.

"Oh. We did so want you to have a good time."

Neither Charlie nor Eve could bring themselves to speak.

"Oh," Cilla said, meaningfully. "Oh."

"Let's have a toast," Marcus said, bringing everyone a glass and filling each with champagne. "Merry Christmas," he began, "and thank God we are strong and healthy and free—"

"And aren't living in Europe in 1943," finished Eve.

They all drank up, except Charles César, who set his glass down on the table.

"Excuse me," he said. "I'm going to mass."

And he went off to get his coat, his beautifully cut jacket flapping behind him.

XVI

It was January and it was freezing. The temperature had been hovering at ten degrees for a week now, and Eve was almost used to it. Mingus, however, was ill, throwing up and listless. She was loath to take him to the vet in such cold, but he was so miserable, she made the appointment. Despite his weakened condition, he fought as she tried to get him into his carrier.

As she struggled with him, trying not to hurt him, trying to push his silky body through the wicker door, she thought about Charlie. Charlie always helped her with this, Charlie held the door open while she dealt with the cat. But Charlie was gone. She was a single woman now, single and forty, the death combination, the stuff of grim cover lines on magazines and tawdry headlines in the tabloids. Woman, Single and Forty Eaten By Rats. Woman, Single and Forty, Hatchets Shrink. Woman, Single and Forty, Worthless Life.

Well, she was in a sad mood, that's all. And stupidly sad at that. It was Charlie who was suffering. My God, Eve thought for the hundredth time as she staggered up the street with the carrier, what could it be like to have catchers for parents? God help him, she prayed, since she couldn't. Elie Wiesel had written that to call the oppressed who are driven to crime "guilty" is wrong. It is taking sides with the oppressor. And Eve had sent Charlie that essay in hopes it would ease him. God only knows what drove them to it, she thought, well, God and the Nazis.

Perhaps, she thought, as she set the carrier on the ground to rest, I am doing wrong by choosing Eva over Charlie. Considering the catchers, considering he is a live person and not a number, considering she loved him and cared about his soul. But something had happened to her, something she couldn't quite define. She had gone cold toward Charlie in some way. When she was with him, she couldn't quite see him anymore, as if he weren't the person she'd thought he was. And when he told her about his parents, that had clinched it. Her heart bled for him in theory, but emotionally she had fled. It was a totally different reaction than she thought she would have to finding out his secrets. She couldn't handle them. They stupefied her. She didn't understand herself at all.

A scrawny, neuralgic woman appeared out of nowhere when she reached the corner. "Isn't it too cold for him?" the woman snapped in a clear accusation of pet abuse.

It never failed, Eve thought. Every time she left the house with the cat carrier, someone appeared to accuse her. Usually Mingus would be yowling, thus creating the impression that the person might be right. Today, however, he was silent, shocked by the cold. Eve was worried about him. She ignored the woman and hailed a cab.

The vet's office was warm and odoriferous. It smelled like disinfectant and dog with a soupçon of cat-litter box thrown in for flavor. It was crowded, as usual, with intense New Yorkers and their child substitutes. It was a funky place with contact-paper-wood walls and cutesy cartoons of talking animals, and framed selections from *Pet Magazine* that someone came and changed once a month. This month's offering was about men and their pets. It said that a study had been done indicating that men were far more affectionate to their pets than they were to their wives and children. Men, it explained, were brought up to show affection primarily to animals, especially their dogs, and that was about it. Any other affection shown was considered wimpy. It was true, Eve thought. Most of her boyfriends were affectionate with her cats, transferring the love they felt for her into their furry souls, still worrying about them after the breakup, decimated when they died. Charles César was the most personally affectionate boyfriend she had ever had but then he was European and Jewish and was indifferent to animals.

There were two park benches for seats in the vet's office, and at the moment they were packed. On one a pudgy, blond girl of about twenty-two cooed to a large, powder-blue cat carrier, and a young, punky guy with a shaved head and an earring, all in black leather, remonstrated with a funky, furless mutt with bad teeth. On the other bench, a nicotine-ridden, bad-tempered gay guy worried over an ulcerous Chihuahua, and a man in a custom-made suit snapped commands at a Doberman pinscher.

Eve put her cat carrier on the floor and leaned against the wall. Mingus yowled and then fell silent. Standing next to her was a scrawny woman in her sixties, the kind that used to live in hole-in-the-wall apartments before the real-estate developers came, cradling something in a towel in her arms.

"Cat?" the woman said, nodding toward Eve's carrier.

"Yes," replied Eve. "Siamese."

"Oh, Siamese. Lovely," the woman replied. "Pigeon"—she went on nodding toward her bundle.

"Pigeon," Eve repeated dully.

"Hit by a taxi, poor lamb," the woman said. "Injured a wing."

"I'm sorry," Eve said.

"Yes, so am I. I feed them every day in Abingdon Square. They have a hell of a time."

The vet came out of the examining room and called the next patient's name. "Motorhead." The punky guy rose and dragged the mutt across the floor.

"Look, Pancho, see. He doesn't want to be here either," the gay guy stage-whispered to his Chihuahua. The animal yapped.

The door opened and a sophisticated black woman entered with a cat carrier. The Doberman pinscher leapt toward her. The owner jerked the dog's collar and snapped, "Heel, sir!" The

Doberman whined.

The black woman checked in at the desk and took the seat left open by the punky guy. Mingus yowled.

"My cat hates the vet," the black woman said. "But she has to have her shots."

"Yes," replied Eve. "Mine hates it, too. They all do, don't they?" She addressed this to the office at large. All the owners nodded. The punky guy and Motorhead emerged from the examining room and the vet called the next patient's name. "Amelia Earhart." The pudgy blond girl picked up her cat carrier and immediately began talking to the vet. "I was using depilatory on my legs and she rubbed against them and now all her fur's come off."

The other pet owners glanced at each other. They were always on the lookout for pet neglect or abuse. Eve picked up Mingus's carrier and sat down on the bench. Mingus yowled piteously as she set him down in front of her feet.

"What's wrong?" the gay guy asked.

"I don't know," said Eve. "I think he's got flu. And yours?" Eve looked down at Pancho, whose eyes were bulging and cloudy from age. The gay guy lit a cigarette with shaky hands, then sucked on it for dear life and replied, "He's an epileptic. Has been for years. What we've been through—Oh God—I couldn't begin—it's just a checkup but I do think he's getting arthritic. I noticed it on Gay Pride Weekend. Usually he just adores walking in the parade. This year I had to carry him. Prima donna. He's worse than Joan Crawford in—in—in anything!" And he guffawed.

The woman with the pigeon addressed the man in the custom-made suit. He wore pitch-black sunglasses and looked to be about thirty-eight. He was clearly uncomfortable in such a low-scale, scruffy setting. The Doberman sat nervously at his feet. Even the biggest, scariest dogs, Eve had observed, cowered at the vet. She wondered if pit bulls did.

"What's wrong?" the pigeon woman asked.

The man delayed a moment before answering. He did not want to talk to her but he finally said dismissively, "Lyme disease."

Everyone gasped. "Really?" The gay guy was fascinated. "Where'd he get that?"

"The Hamptons," the man snapped.

"Christ on a crutch." The gay guy crossed himself. "There are some good things about being poverty-stricken, Pancho. At least we don't go anywhere you can get Lyme disease."

"Do you think that pit bulls are the Gestapo of dogs?" Eve asked the black woman sitting next to her. The woman was stunning, sleek and well dressed, with flawless brown skin and sloe eyes. The woman looked confused.

"The what?" she replied.

"The Gestapo," Eve repeated.

"I don't know what that means. What is that "Gestapo'?" she asked.

"Oh." Eve was taken by surprise. She tried to be succinct. "They were the secret police of the Nazi regime in Germany during World War Two."

"Oh," the black woman thought for a moment. "Oh, yes. Oh, yes, then in answer to your question, yes, pit bulls are."

"Pit bulls get a bum rap," the man in the custom-made suit suddenly said.

Everyone looked at him.

"Oh, really," the gay guy was sarcastic. The Doberman bared his teeth. "Dobermans were the Gestapo of dogs, weren't they?" the gay guy added. The man kept silent beneath his sunglasses.

The phone rang and the girl at the reception desk began to take down information. Catchers, Eve thought to herself, as in dog catchers.

In a book about daily life in the Third Reich, she had read of a woman who, upon entering a hotel restaurant, was greeted by three signs: WOMEN WITH RED TALONS AND TROUSERS ARE FORBIDDEN. HEIL HITLER IS THE PRESCRIBED GREETING. and DOGS AND JEWS NOT ALLOWED. And that about said it in a nutshell. But what kind of world would embrace such overt hatred? Sometimes people in their seventies and eighties would tell Eve how sweet life used to be, how little crime there was, how much fellowship people had in the twenties and thirties and Eve would reply, "Yes. That was the sweet innocent world that brought us Jim Crow and the holocaust. A world in which racial hatred flowered and slavery was fun. In which eugenics was accepted as science. Yes, incredible innocence.

The vet came out of the examining room followed by the pudgy blond girl hugging the powder-blue cat carrier. The girl was crying. "It'll grow back," the vet was saying. "It'll grow back." The girl went up to the reception desk to pay and the vet took the next card and called out the patient's name.

"Pancho," the vet called. The gay guy jumped and stubbed out his cigarette.

"Come on, darling," the gay guy said, but Pancho cringed and slunk under the bench. "Pancho," the gay guy's tone was mildly threatening. "Pancho!" The gay guy was annoyed. He pulled on Pancho's leash but to no avail. The dog whimpered and clung to the bench. The gay guy bent down and, with his shaking hands, picked up Pancho and kissed him on the cheek. "How do you think Daddy feels when he has to go for his blood test every six months? And Daddy doesn't behave this way. Get your ass in there, Mary." The gay guy laughed raucously and twitched Pancho into the examining room.

Eve opened the top of her cat carrier and peered in at Mingus. His myopic Siamese face peered back at her. "Hi, Mingee," she murmured and stroked his head. She pulled out her hand, refastened the carrier, and the pigeon lady said, "What's that?" She was referring to the tattoo which, during the previous maneuver, had become visible.

"What?" asked Eve.

"That," the pigeon lady pointed with her bundle at Eve's arm.

The black woman followed the pigeon lady's gesture and saw the tattoo. Curious, she waited for Eve's answer. The man in the custom-made suit turned his head Eve's way. Of course, his glasses were so dark, no one could see what he saw. The receptionist was busy on the phone and saw nothing.

"Oh," said Eve, taking her time. She wasn't quite prepared for an enlightenment. Usually she had one in her mind when she left the house, but what with all the flurry of getting Mingus in the box . . .

"It's the prisoner I.D. number of a woman who was at Auschwitz. Her name was Eva Beck."

The pigeon lady grew somber and backed away a bit. The black woman was surprised.

"Why are you wearing that?" she asked with some distaste.

"I'm wearing it in remembrance, or like an MIA bracelet."

"I know nothing about that stuff," the black woman said. "I guess a lot of Jews died."

"A lot of Jews died," Eve replied. "A lot of all kinds of people died. The concept of inferior race became all-encompassing. Initially though, a lot of Nazi racial programs and ideology were modeled on American ones at the time. The Nazis thoroughly approved of American segregational laws.

"Really," the black woman said. "I bet. Ain't that interesting. You Jewish?" the black woman asked.

"That's an interesting question." Eve sized her up and decided to lie. "You tell me. I'm baptized Catholic, confirmed Episcopalian, my mother's family is Irish Catholic, priests and nuns, my father's family was Jewish but never practiced the religion. Under Nazi law I'm *Mischlinge* in the first degree. That's half-breed in the first degree: two Jewish grandparents. I might not be considered Jewish if I were married to a non-Jew and had non-Jewish children and if I didn't look Jewish. If I looked Jewish, then under Nazi law, thank you, I would be considered Jewish. That is the science of racial eugenics for you."

"You don't look Jewish," the black woman said.

"No," said Eve. "So they tell me."

"Who was Eva Beck?" the pigeon lady asked.

In the examining room, Pancho was yapping. The phones at the reception desk were ringing off the hook. Mingus sang out a querulous yowl. Eve looked from the pigeon lady to the black woman and began.

Eva Beck was a woman around forty who loved animals, Eve told them. She lived on the outskirts of the city in an apartment containing ten dogs and cats, several fish, and a giant cage of finches. Eva was unmarried and no longer worked. Sometimes her brother gave her money. Sometimes she did odd jobs around the neighborhood, a little baby-sitting here, some mending there, but people didn't trust her. Ever since the Citizenship Law had been passed in '35, which said that unmarried women were not citizens but inhabitants of the Reich, the neighbors had realized that she was a bit odd. What could be going on in the mind of a woman without a husband or children, they asked themselves. It's a failure of duty, some said. She must be crazy, others pronounced. Her family stayed away from her, all except her brother, who only came when she really needed him.

The truth was actually rather simple. Eva had picked the wrong men. Mean men. Men who had treated her badly. Men who had left her after making false promises. And then one day, she stopped seeing men altogether. It was the Weimar period and she got heavily involved in Women's Emancipation, and for a long time, she was happy. She excelled at her work, became office manager for the firm that employed her, rented a large apartment for herself and her animals, and then Hitler came to power. As women could no longer hold managerial positions, she was fired, and then the Reich Citizenship Law was enacted, and she found herself unemployed, without money, and the object of fear and pity. She considered having a child to save herself from complete ignominy. But that meant sleeping with men. She decided against it.

For a long time she isolated herself, living like a hermit, with only her animals for comfort. She could have gotten another job, but she had no energy for it. She could drag herself out of bed only to feed her pets. They were the only creatures she cared about in the world. She let her appearance go, and began to look, her family told her, like a bum. Her neighbors noticed her decline, but they practiced a live-and-let-live policy toward her because they respected her brother. Everything was fine until the Jewish Pet Collection Center was established in the Parish Council building across from where she lived.

One day in 1940, Eva was walking up her street when she came upon an amazing sight. Streaming out of the Parish Council building, winding around two city blocks and beyond, was a long line of well-dressed people holding animals. Dogs and cats, bird cages and fish bowls, monkeys and lemurs, some on leashes, some in carriers, some in arms. She even espied a wolf cub, an eagle, and several boa constrictors. The sound emanating from the line was cacophonous, a mélange of barks and mews, caws and hisses, human conversation, moans, and tears. The movement along the line was bizarre, both erratic and precise, the struggles of hundreds of animals in close proximity to each other, sensing trouble and pulling against the owners that had them tethered.

It was like a strange motion picture, Eva thought. And for a while she stood there enjoying the cutest of the animals, some Dalmatian puppies strung together with rope, a high-bred Siamese cat on a velvet leash, until finally her attention strayed to the strained faces of their owners, and she realized this was something ominous. Some policemen stood supervising the line and Eva sidled over to one that she knew and asked, "Hey, Karl. What is this?"

"Jews," Karl replied. "About to be deported. They must turn in their pets."

"And what happens to those pets?" Eva asked, sensing the worst.

"I don't know," said Karl, and he looked away guiltily.

It was at that moment that the revolutionary in Eva was born.

Eva rushed away, down the line, until she reached a spot where no policemen were in evidence. Here, a stretch of twenty people stood surrounded by their pets. She surveyed the animals carefully. There was a young German shepherd, three Persian cats in boxes, two weimaraners, four parrots in cages, four dachshunds, three Dobermans, and two bowls of fish, regular gold and exotic fighting. Eva walked up and down the line, calculating in her mind, observing the animals' behavior. Finally she selected what she observed to be the healthiest dog and the most docile cat, and she walked over to their owners.

"Pardon me," she said to the owner of one of the Dobermans. "Come over here."

The owner, a well-dressed man in his mid-forties wearing a Star of David armband, regarded her nervously.

"Don't be afraid," she whispered. "I want to help you." The man hesitated and then moved away from the line and stood by her.

"They intend to take your dog and kill it," she said bluntly.

The man sagged.

"Give the dog to me and I will save his life."

She stared at the man and he stared back. She looked around her. There were still no policemen in sight.

"Quickly," she added.

The man handed her the leash.

Eva took the dog and walked briskly down the line to a young woman holding a wooden cat carrier.

"Pardon me," she began. "They are not trustworthy. Give me your cat and I will save her life," she said.

The young woman burst into tears.

"Shush," Eva hissed. "Shush. You can come get her after the war. I live in that red house up the street. Beck. Can you remember that?"

"No," the young woman protested. "No."

"Please," Eva pleaded. The woman was weeping copiously now. The others in the line were becoming curious. Eva turned on her heel and walked away.

"Wait"—the young woman ran after her. "Here, Beck," she said and handed Eva the cat carrier.

Eva took hold of it and, with the Doberman pulling her forward, hobbled off down an alley and away from the street.

The next day, Eva sneaked into the pet collection center and surveyed the scene. In this giant room, three long tables were set up, behind which three SS men checked in the Jewish pets and then handed them to orderlies who stacked and tied them inside two huge cages provided for the purpose. The sound of barking and yowling and yapping and hissing echoed off the walls. If a dog became hysterical, the orderly would bop it with a truncheon and knock it out. The smell of animal feces and urine permeated the air. Eva was so horrified by what she saw that she almost fainted.

In the next few weeks, Eva tried to save as many dogs and cats as she could. The birds she took and let loose in the park not too far from her house. Pretty soon her rooms were filled top to bottom with animals and she was in a bind. She tried to give some animals away but, what with rationing, there was little food for pets and no one wanted them. Then she had an idea.

One day when she had collected six excellent-quality Dobermans, she put on her best dress and hat and walked to Gestapo headquarters in Prinz Albrechtstrasse and spoke to the SS man in reception.

"Pardon," she began rather snootily. "I am Eva Beck, breeder of dogs, and I would like to sell these Dobermans into your service. They are fine watchdogs or whatever you wish them for—"

She looked down her nose at the SS man.

"One moment," he replied, and he called someone on his telephone. In a few moments, another SS man appeared and examined the Dobermans.

"Have they papers?" he asked.

Eva panicked. "Yes, of course," she covered. And if you are interested, I shall bring them."

The SS man made a call on his telephone.

"All right," he said. "How much?"

Eva smiled and named her price. The SS man agreed and took the dogs.

"Bring their papers tomorrow," he said.

Eva nodded.

On the way home, Eva was triumphant. She took some of the money and walked around her neighborhood until she spied Hans Rohr, the local forger, standing in front of a tavern.

Hans was a strange young man, scarred from smallpox, and a minor criminal. The war had made him rich. He was a scion of the black market, purveyor of everything, especially identification documents and forged papers.

"Hans," Eva whispered. "I have a job for you. Top secret."

Hans snickered. Eva was well known in the neighborhood as a crazy spinster, an animal nut. Just last week, he had spoken with her landlady. Eva had gone berserk, the woman said, with the strays. It was driving the building to mania. The smell was something terrible. It was quite possible Eva would be evicted.

"Yeah, what?" Hans replied.

"I need some papers," Eva said.

Hans was intrigued. "Going somewhere?" he asked. "Jews?"

"No, no, no," Eva sniffed. "Nothing like that. Fake breeding papers for Dobermans. Highfalutin family trees. I have money."

She flashed a wad of bills. Hans laughed.

"Breeding papers for dogs? I've never done such a job."

"I'm sure you can do it," she said. "For a price, you'll do anything."

"That's correct, lady," he answered, grinning.

"I need them tomorrow. Six different family trees, and there will be more." She said this as if holding out a huge carrot for a horse.

"Okay." He laughed. "Okay. It'll be fun."

The next day Eva took the papers to the SS man and he was very pleased.

"Ah, Grand Champion Reichsführer, out of Eva Braun, we've never had a strain this pure," he cooed. Eva smiled. This was Hans's little joke. "And on the father's side, Franklin and Eleanor Roosevelt. Very political. Very amusing."

After this Eva kept up a steady flow of "pure" dogs to the SS. She also interested them in "purebred" cats. But though she was making money and saving dogs and cats of excellence, her heart broke for the strays and mutts she could not select and she decided to save those on alternate days and take home. She stopped doing odd jobs around the neighborhood and began to get a reputation for hanging around on streetcorners with the likes of Hans.

Eva's landlady was fit to be tied. She was getting her rent on time, but she was disgusted by Eva's life-style. There were constant complaints about the smell and the noise and, it was said, Eva was becoming crazier, more furtive and hostile, showing, perhaps, the innate subhuman characteristics that had kept her unmarried and childless.

One day early in 1941, when Eva was standing on a streetcorner awaiting Hans, she was arrested in a roundup of the asocial and work-shy. She was charged under the Community Alien Law of 1940, which stated that "a person is alien to the community if he/she proves to be incapable of satisfying the minimum requirements of the national community through his/her own efforts, in particular through an unusual degree of deficiency of mind or character." Her landlady, of course, had turned her in.

While at Gestapo headquarters, she was sighted by the SS man with whom she did business and her entire operation was uncovered.

Jewish pets. The SS man shook his head. "You sold the Gestapo Jewish pets. Well, this proves what we have always suspected: the Jews have always hoarded the best pets. And he made sure she was sent to Auschwitz. Eva died there while doing hard labor in 1942.

Eve fell silent. The pigeon lady and the black woman were both weeping quietly. The man in the custom-made suit bowed his head. The vet came out of the examining room followed by the gay man dragging Pancho behind him.

"Arthritis," the gay man announced to the waiting room. "I was right."

"Billie Holiday," the vet called out.

The black woman rose and hauled her cat carrier into the examining room. A moment passed and there was a terrible animal scream. Hissing, spitting, screaming, yowling. The vet cried out, "I need help in here."

The receptionist jumped from her seat and, grabbing some long, thick gloves, disappeared around the corner.

The animals in the waiting room cowered and shrank. The humans looked at each other in fear and held their heads. After some minutes of tortuous screaming and agony, the black woman reappeared with her cat carrier in the waiting room.

"Next time, I think I'll skip the shots," she said.

XVII

It was morning and the Village was shimmering in the pure, white light of winter. Eve was on her way to the Dolphin Café to have coffee before she began to write. Her routine had changed completely now that Charlie was gone. It was all about herself. She did not cook or clean for anybody else, or accept invitations on anyone else's behalf. Her typewriter was out of the closet now, sitting out on the table for everyone to see. She wrote when she felt like it, thought when she felt like it, read when the fancy struck her. She reported only to Mingus who was recovering from his flu, and, of course, to Eva.

Her new independence pleased her. She felt stronger, solid, and free. But, oh, how she missed loving Charlie. She passed the Chinese laundry and wished she were taking his shirts there. She darted by the pharmacy and ached to buy him after-shave. In window after window, she saw presents he would like, presents that would make him laugh, and she fantasized his coming through the door and throwing her arms around him, and just staying there encircled by his warmth until she melted away. The wifely part of Eve, neglected and in mourning, was wizening. A person could go mad not being allowed to love, she thought to herself.

She rounded the corner by the bank, and a violent noise at the end of the street caught her attention. She stopped dead, as did other pedestrians around her, and stared in the direction of the sounds, ready to run.

A block away, a homeless black man was flailing and shouting. A white employee of the Korean deli rushed out of the store, shouting, too, and began beating the homeless man with a stick.

"My God," cried Eve.

"Oh, please, does it have to be like this every morning?" a young woman near her moaned.

"You know, I paid three hundred thousand dollars to live in the fucking projects here," a young man commented to Eve.

He turned to the young woman and, rifling his pocket for money, removed some bills and gave them to her.

"Take a taxi, honey," he said. "Forget the bus. Why don't they put those fuckers in the loony bin where they belong?" He addressed this last to Eve and, when she didn't reply, the anger in his eyes dispersed. "I'm sorry," he said brusquely.

They were all scared. He took the young woman out into the street and hailed a cab for her. Then he fled toward the subway.

Eve looked up. The shouting had become screaming now. The homeless man ran away from the deli guy, across the avenue into the pocket park where his cart waited. The cart was overflowing with items, among them a mop handle, which the homeless man grabbed. He ran out of the pocket park onto the avenue and lurched forward. A fat, middle-aged black lady stepped out of his way and proceeded on, followed, some steps beyond, by a studious-looking white guy in an anorak, sporting glasses and a beard. The homeless guy swung the mop handle like a bat, and whacked the bearded guy on the back. Eve cried out. The bearded man fell onto a parked car. The homeless guy continued on, swinging at every white person he passed.

Eve ran across the avenue and helped the bearded man to his feet.

"Are you all right?" she asked.

The man was in shock. "Yes," he mumbled.

"He was fighting with that deli guy." She pointed at the Korean deli. "Are you sure?"

"I think so," the man replied, feeling his ribs.

"Okay. Take care of yourself today. Pay attention to yourself," Eve said.

"Thank you for your interest." The man sounded surprised.

Eve shrugged and turned back toward the Dolphin Café. She took a deep breath. She was shaking. She flew up the avenue saying to herself, I never want to see that again. I never want to see a man beating another man with a stick. No.

The area around the Korean deli was unusually quiet now. The aftermath of street violence in life was nothing like its depiction on TV. On TV sirens blared, people ran and shouted, all was excitement and furor. In life, there was silence. Silence, sadness, and shock. Eve passed some neighbors speaking urgently to each other but quietly. There was a deadness in the air. It depressed most humans to see other humans suffer. It depressed most humans to see other humans die. And police sirens depressed most humans, too. It was almost genetic fact.

Eve reached the Korean deli and stopped. The white deli guy was still outside. He was gathering up the oranges that the homeless man had scattered on the ground. He was muttering with rage.

"This is the fifth fuckin' time! Five fuckin'—"

"You can't beat people with sticks," Eve said to him. "I don't care. You can't."

"Fuck you," the deli guy replied.

She nodded in acquiescence and stepped off the curb onto the avenue.

"Fuck you," the deli guy shouted after her.

As Eve waited for the light, she wondered about Eva. How many scenes of street violence had Eva witnessed, had Eva been part of? Once Eve had seen a photo of Nazi street violence in Berlin. In it, a Jewish woman, about Eva's age, was caught, naked, surrounded by taunting SS men. The look of sheer terror

124

on the woman's face, her nakedness in the street, her absolute vulnerability, was something that Eve would never forget. Another of the reasons she'd gotten the tattoo. She prayed that hadn't happened to Eva.

Before Eve left the house, she had been reading more about the Euthanasia Program. She was searching for every fact she could get on it and, that morning, she'd found one that had stopped her in her tracks. It seemed that the first mass gassing chamber, the one for German mental patients, had been designed as a shower. As each patient entered the shower, he or she was stamped with a rubber stamp on which was inked an I.D. number, a proto-tattoo. In other words, Eve thought, the entire lying design was conceived to kill worthless Aryan life. And the whole process of mass killing was in full swing two years before the extermination of the Jews was ordered at the Wannsee Conference in 1942. In fact, initially, Jewish mental patients were barred from euthanasia. The Nazis said they did not deserve it.

The Euthanasia Program, Eve read, was an outgrowth of the "racial science" of the twenties and thirties. A twisted combination of social Darwinism, physical anthropology, and Lamarckian theory, racial science had taken hold throughout the world, in America as well. The Nazis had not thought up the murder and sterilization of "worthless life" but they were the first government to back the theories as fact, embrace them as a national ethic, and constitute them into immutable law. Presumably, Eve thought, a good part of the German populace believed in racial theory. What they didn't quite get was the difference between theory and law.

It didn't surprise Eve that the Nazis kept the Euthanasia Program secret, just as later they tried to keep the gassing of Jews secret. But she read that as Germans caught on to the fake death certificates, and became aware that their relatives were being murdered, there was an outcry. German Catholics staged a demonstration. The Euthanasia Program was officially halted in August of 1941, by which time 70,273 Germans had been gassed. Killing by other methods, however, continued at various mental institutions until the end of the war. When the program was officially stopped in '41, the gassing showers were dismantled, packed up, and shipped from the mental institutions to the concentration camps, where they became the infamous showers of the holocaust.

No matter what the Nazis claimed, Eve thought as she crossed the avenue, the killing of "worthless Aryan life" was not about killing another race. It was a self-disembowelment. It reminded her of a man she had read about in the newspaper who was taken to a hospital when he tried to perform an appendectomy on himself and failed. When the doctors operated on him, they found this was not his first procedure, he had already removed his own spleen.

At the time, Eve recalled, she was flabbergasted. It had never occurred to her that such a perversion existed. Operating on oneself? For what? Sexual excitement? It was so blood-and-guts sick, she couldn't stand it.

She was struck in the same way by the Euthanasia Program, and wondered why there had been so little focus on it. The killing of "other" was a tradition in human history. The killing of "self" was new. Surely this first mass killing of "worthless self" was intricately connected to the mass killing of "other" in Nazi Germany. Surely in understanding why mass murder of other, one had to understand this self-murder first. Could you have had self without other? Would you have had other without self?

"He's a little swine, that one." The waitress at the Dolphin stood in the doorway. She was referring to the white deli guy who was still screaming at Eve, still brandishing the stick.

"Maybe he hates to see their misery so much, he wants to kill them," said Eve. "They remind him of himself."

"And he's a swine," the waitress said. "Trip-hammer temper. Does it to his wife, too, I'd venture. The usual?"

Eve nodded and entered the Dolphin. The waitress padded to
126 the kitchen.

"I'd like to machine-gun every one of those loonies," Mike said, baiting her.

He was leaning over her table. Mike owned the Dolphin. He was young, bright, conservative, and round as a top. In spite of the image he cast for himself he was good-hearted and jolly.

"Yes, well," answered Eve, "of course once you start beating people with sticks or machine-gunning them, as you prefer, you do realize you've descended to subhumanity? Once you dehumanize one part of the society, the rest becomes dehumanized as well."

Mike looked abashed. Eve felt odd. The way she spoke out now brought her a different reaction than she was used to. Once men feared her writing voice, she told Eva, now they were afraid of her. She touched the tattoo to calm herself. She and Eva were off duty in the mornings. Mike had never seen the tattoo.

"Listen," he said, " 'couple of weeks ago, one of the loonies smashed a bottle outside and tried to cut me with it. Just went off, screaming, wacko, and I got the bat. Along comes a writer for one of those lefty papers, sees me defending myself, and attacks *me!* There's no cops. You tell me. What am I supposed to do?"

"I don't know. Get a psycho net," said Eve.

"Good idea." Mike grinned. "I should get one free for the taxes I pay. Look at that guy. Look at him. There's trouble."

Mike was pointing at a homeless man who was loitering outside the Dolphin, near the door. The man was huge, with deep black skin and insanely matted, long hair. He wore many ill-fitting coats, all misbuttoned, and plastic boots with holes in them. He was filthy, the dirt caked on his face and clothing, and streaked, like eyeliner, around his blood-red eyes.

"I just think of them as another race now," Mike said, looking out the window at the man. "C'mon, Eve, look at him. He's suffered some mutation in his cells. Could you live like that?"

" 'The quality of mercy is not strained. It droppeth as the gentle rain from—' "

"You're such a liberal, Eve. Bleeding heart."

"When did having a heart become a detriment in this country, can you tell me?" Eve was furious.

"Look," Mike began but he was cut off by a percussive explosion so thunderous, it threw him across the restaurant and whiplashed Eve back against the booth and onto the floor. Before her eyes, the two front plate-glass windows melted and slid to the ground. There was a beat of silence and then Mike shouted and rushed out the door. The homeless man, who was looking up at the sky, whirled around and shoved Mike as hard as he could away from the doorway. A manhole cover as big as a tire fell down from above and clanged onto the doorsill. In shock, Mike glanced at the homeless man, then at the manhole cover, and then rushed back into the restaurant.

"Is everyone all right?" Mike shouted.

Eve could barely hear him. She got herself up off the floor and dusted herself off.

Mike was on the phone.

"Hi." His voice was high and faint. "Dolphin Café. Hudson and Bank. A manhole cover just blew. Get some people over here—what?" He turned to Eve. "They want me to hold."

Eve laughed. Her head hurt. She walked slowly to the door. Her body was working. She was all right. The waitress was standing in the doorway, crying. She was young and new to the city. The busboy, who was Cuban, was shaking and praying.

Behind them, Mike was shouting, "Hudson and Bank! Hudson and Bank! For Christ's sake—Mike Reilly—I own the place! I'll be here! Unfuckingbelievable!"

He slammed down the phone and redialed.

"Ted. Ted, a manhole cover just blew and shattered my windows. Damn right, sue! Get over here, would ya? Thanks."

Mike ran past Eve and out onto the avenue. He was darting to and fro among the other store owners who had congregated on the pavement around the manhole cover. The homeless guy was walking in circles muttering to himself.

128 "Nothing works. Nothing works." The homeless man began

to scream it. The store owners turned as a group and looked at him.

"Someone's making sense," the waitress said.

Mike went off. "Get the fuck out of here! Get the fuck away!" He ran toward the homeless man.

"Mike," Eve shouted. "He saved your life!"

Mike stopped and reddened. He went to pat the guy on the shoulder but couldn't bring himself to touch him. He used his hands to gesture instead. "I'm sorry, okay. I'm sorry. Thanks. Relax."

Mike sheepishly went back to the crowd of store owners. Sirens blared up the street and three police cars drove up and parked.

"Don't cry, honey," Eve took the waitress's hand. "We're all okay. We're safe."

Eve moved the waitress and the busboy out onto the sidewalk. The Arab newsstand owner was wailing and gesticulating to the stone-faced Korean guy who owned the deli.

"It is like Beirut now! Bombs! Maniacs!"

His younger brother, who worked in the newsstand and who was standing by his side, said quietly, "No. Even now it is not like Beirut."

The Korean guy nodded in assent. He had no idea what Beirut was.

"Animals!" the Korean guy hissed.

"Animals!" the Arabs echoed.

One of the Russian ladies who worked in the leg-waxing and nail parlor turned to Eve and said sotto voce, "In the morning when we come to work, the drug people and the prostitutes are hanging around in front of the store—terrible. They look like devils. In Russia we never saw this. We don't understand. Such a beautiful, rich country. We—"

A herd of sirens crescendoed around them and more police cars drove up. Another herd of Con Ed vans arrived and parked.

Now it was like TV, Eve thought, as long as no one was hurt.

A woman with a dog loitered on the fringes of the crowd. A

young woman jogger ran up beside her and stopped, removing her headphones. "What's going on?" she asked.

"You name it," the woman replied.

"You know what I really think?" the young woman said.

"What?" the woman gentled her dog, who had begun to snarl at the Arabs.

"It's all the fault of pornography. The whole damn thing. I'm leaving this city."

"Really," the woman looked very interested. "Me, too. Where you moving to?"

"Vermont," the young woman said. "And you?"

"Santa Fe," the woman replied.

Out of the crowd of Villagers who had collected behind them, different place names now rang out.

"Key West."

"Tucson."

"Europe."

"Denver."

"Berlin."

They were in a reverie now, all of them, calling out their dream places, their eyes glazed over with the drug of escape.

Eve surveyed the waitress. "How old are you?" she asked.

"Twenty-three," the waitress replied.

What can it be like to be twenty-three in this violent world? Eve thought to herself. Then she asked this question aloud.

Through her tears the waitress laughed. "Aw, I'm used to it. It's fine. It's all I know. I don't think about it."

The cacophony around them was mind-boggling. The pretty gypsy wife from the fortune-telling parlor trotted up now, followed by her four-year-old son Jimmy, who was adorable but, as the gypsy put it, "an Indian."

"Hi, Mary," Eve knew the gypsy. She was an astute reader. Eve almost went to her after Charles César left, but she thought better of it. She knew, if she cared to know it, all there was to tell.

"What's up?" Mary said. "Was it those Arabs?"

She meant terrorists.

"No, a manhole cover blew."

Mary didn't understand. Eve pointed to the metal saucer on the pavement, around which the Con Ed guys and police were having a conference.

"Ohhhhhh." Mary's eyes widened. "You mean those blow up? I walked on those wit my kids."

Little Jimmy, who was carrying a can of Crazy String, now sprayed it on the elder Arab newsstand dealer, who bellowed at the top of his lungs. The cops jerked toward him and then laughed. Seething, the man walked toward Mary and Eve, his mouth set, his eyes burning. His head was covered with neon-pink strands of whatever weird stuff the toy was made of.

"I will not stand for this," he snarled at Mary. "You watch him. If this happens again, I will——"

Mary threw up her hands in mock despair. "I'm sorry. He's an Indian," she said, stifling a smile.

"Jimmeeee," she called to the boy, who was running in circles around the crowd. She shouted some admonition in Hungarian. The Russian ladies seemed to understand what she said and laughed to themselves. The Arab stalked away in a fury.

"It comes right off," Eve called after him.

"He's not a good person," Mary said knowingly. She shook her head.

"What's up, Mary?" Eve asked. She meant psychically.

Mary rolled her eyes.

"This is some times. I don't like it. I don't see this before."

"Well, Eastern Europe's a positive thing, don't you think?" Eve asked.

Mary beamed for a moment and then fell serious. "Bless Jesus," she intoned. "But I don't got no family there anymore, so . . ."

Eve took a chance. Generally she didn't press the gypsy for information other than spiritual, but since they were speaking as neighbors, she made a stab.

"No one in Hungary?"

131

"No," Mary replied soberly. "Those Nazis killed them all. Thirty-five peoples in my family. See those women?"

She pointed at the Russian ladies.

"Those Nazis killed their families too. Can you believe this? Small world, huh? They told me this once when I got my nails wrapped. They did it for me for free. I read them sometimes. They's had a hard life."

Eve stared at the three Russian ladies. They were all large-boned people, all in their late forties, all with set, grim faces. They had each waxed her legs on occasion, and when she asked them about Gorbachev, glasnost, and perestroika, they had each laughed cynically.

"Don't believe anything that comes out of that rotten society," they cautioned as one. "Lies. All lies."

Mary grabbed Jimmy as he ran by and held him.

"Yah," she said, "my family used to dance for them in the camps. They played music and danced for them but it didn't save them, though."

"Mary," Eve said, "I found something out. Charlie's Jewish."

Mary's eyes sparkled.

"Oh, yah?" she asked. "That's good for you. Those Jews have some powers."

Eve looked at her questioningly.

"Come see me." She took Jimmy's hand. "Come for a reading. I see maybe your aura's a little weak."

And she turned and strolled back to her storefront with Jimmy laughing and chortling beside her.

Eve stood back from the crowd and surveyed the scene. All the people before her had their lives changed by the cataclysm that was World War II, and she bet they hardly thought about it. Perhaps, the only way human beings could continue to reproduce was by practicing selective memory. It was much the same with old people. She felt their loss of memory was somehow merciful, somehow soothing to their decrepit bodies. They seemed to remember only the incidents they really wanted to, the way they wanted to. What use the minutiae of life that makes one's adrenaline rise when one is young?

And here were the Nazis again, where she least expected them, but where she ought to have known they would be, loitering ghosts in a crowd of Americans who had never even seen one.

"Eve?"

Cheryl, the young wife of the man who owned the Italian restaurant across from her building, stood above her. She was leaning on a stroller that was barely containing her two-year-old.

"Are you okay?"

Eve nodded, then smiled.

"Can you believe?" Cheryl asked.

"Momeeeee," the two-year-old was screaming at the top of her lungs.

"Shush," Cheryl said and closed her eyes. "Please shush."

"How's business?" Eve asked.

The two-year-old was flinging herself against the stroller seat belt, twisting and lurching, making a lot of noise. Cheryl raised her voice. "Not so hot. Not so hot for anyone. My older daughter's in school in the mornings. At St. Joan's. Guess how much it costs? Ten thousand bucks."

Cheryl laughed.

"Terrifying," said Eve. "What about public school?"

"No good," Cheryl said definitively.

"Cheryl, she's playing with blocks. I didn't have a coherent thought until sixth grade."

"I know. I know. But, you know——" Cheryl gestured at the scene around them. "It's a matter of protection. For ten thousand bucks, maybe a manhole cover won't blow in the vicinity of the school. Maybe a berserk vet won't open up on the playground. Maybe . . ."

"Momeeeee," the two-year-old was bellowing. Then she began to sob. Hysterical crying, with huge, heart-rending sobs.

"Okay. Okay. Come here," Cheryl said wearily. She bent down and unhooked the struggling baby from the seat belt. The child was out of control, kicking and spitting, screaming at a level that made them both cower. Eve flashed on Eva Klein, hunted and weary.

"Please," Cheryl was saying to the baby, "we're going home. We're going home."

She pushed off, wielding the fighting baby, gesturing to Eve with a little hand wave. Eve turned back to the Dolphin. The police cars were pulling away. The crowd was dispersing. The store owners were returning to their stores. Mike was inside shouting at Ted, his lawyer. The homeless man was shuffling back to his bench in the pocket park across the avenue. All that remained outside were two Con Ed trucks, a barricade around the manhole, and the waitress and busboy sweeping up shards of glass that shimmered in the cold winter light like discarded riches.

XVIII

In February, Eve crashed the opening of Charles César's movie. She wore a long-sleeved woolen dress so as to cover the tattoo in case she saw him. She told Eva she wasn't really going in order to see him. She just couldn't not be there at the opening of his film. It was too sad.

She left the house late, hoping to arrive just as the film was beginning but, unfortunately, when she walked into the Soho theater lobby, it was still packed with people. It seemed that the projectionist had been mugged on the way to work and needed some time to recover.

"What are you doing here?"

It was Babe. She had suddenly appeared out of the crowd.

"I'm crashing," Eve said.

Babe was pleased by this.

"Can you believe?" Babe asked. "Thank God the projectionist wasn't murdered or we'd be standing here all night talking about the disenfranchised."

"Only the tenor would be a little different," Eve replied.

Eve and Babe surveyed the lobby. It was filled with documentary filmmakers dressed in the dowdy, cheap clothing favored by the workers about whom they made films. Most of them had gone to Harvard, Yale, or NYU film school, but they visited the upscale salons of their youth only when they raised money. In this crowd, Charlie always looked like a backer.

"There," said Babe, cocking an eye, "Mary Winston. She's making a film she describes as a 'witty, irreverent look at menopause.' "

Eve did a take.

"I suppose it's possible," mused Babe.

"Do you?" asked Eve. "What do you hear about Charlie's film?"

"I hear it's good. The timing's kind of strange, now that we're in love with the Russkies."

"Yes. I've been meaning to ask: Will you be going back to Minsk to find your roots?"

"You bet. Minsk. Lodz. Vilna. All the magical places my parents spoke so spellbindingly about. I once asked my grandfather why he never traveled to Europe. He said, 'I've been to Europe.' His mother was murdered in a pogrom."

"I guess you're thrilled then about the opening up of Eastern Europe, and the possible reunification of Germany."

"Thrilled is close."

"Go back, Babe. Forgive."

"I'm working on it in therapy."

Across the lobby, Eve saw Charles César. He was proud and happy, she could tell. He was wearing a beautiful light gray suit and his Italian leather moccasins, his lucky moccasins, on his small, aristocratic feet. He was in rapt conversation with a plain girl in glasses, dowdily dressed like the crowd around her, only foreignly dowdy. He looked like a young king in audience with a commoner until he took the girl's hand.

"Who's that?" Eve snapped.

"Who?" asked Babe.

"With Charlie, over there."

"Oh," Babe said.

Eve stared her down.

"He didn't expect you to be here."

"All my friends are here," Eve said. "Who is it?"

Babe sighed.

"It's the new girlfriend, Louise Kowalski. A Polish-Jewish filmmaker."

"Jewish?" Eve focused on the woman across the lobby. "Really?" she asked sadly.

Tears came to her eyes. Babe took her hand.

"He loves you. If only you'd get rid of my mother's favorite topic—"

She meant the tattoo. Eve shook her head angrily. She was packed in like a sardine. She was beginning to feel faint.

"It's an infatuation," Babe went on. "The woman cares deeply about man and Yahweh and mushrooms."

"You know," Eve said, "I always thought Charlie looked like a Catholic priest, a member of the high clergy, like a cardinal."

Babe scrutinized him. "The church turns you on?" she asked.

"Yes," Eve replied.

"You're right. He does. A very sexy, aristocratic priest."

"No, he doesn't," Eve said. "Not anymore."

"C'mon, lambkin," said Babe, "let's talk about something cheerful."

Babe took Eve by the shoulders and turned her around so her back was to Charles César.

"Now," she said, "tell me about the tattoo. What have you found out?"

After the dinner party, Babe had taken an interest in Eve's investigation of the women. "It's a dirty job," Babe had told her, "but somebody's got to do it."

"Well," Eve began. She felt woozy. "I found out something interesting about Hitler. He was handsome when he was young."

"You're kidding," said Babe. "He always looks like a pig in those documentaries."

"I know. I couldn't figure out the attraction but then, finally, I saw this biography on TV and they had pictures of him around 1928. Babe, he was really good looking. And they showed one of his rallies, right from the beginning, not just the part where he's screaming, and I could see it, Babe. He had a little Alan Bates, a little Anthony Newley, and a soupçon of Fredric March. He *was* attractive to women. I believe it now."

"Hitler turned you on?" Babe grinned.

"For a split second, yes. You know, Hitler always said that Germany was his bride. Well, he was the worst husband Germany ever had."

"A wife abuser?" asked Babe.

"Yes. He told the women he wanted earth mothers, unpainted childbearers, hippie mamas, you know? And the whole time he was cheating on them with Eva Braun, a makeup-wearing bimbo who changed her designer frock twice a day. Classic."

"The women didn't know about Eva?"

"No. They would have dumped him if they'd known. The woman he loved was an unmarried, childless fashion plate, by law not good enough to be a citizen of the Reich."

"Amazing. As you say, classic."

"So, first he got the women through sexual attraction. Sex, Babe, it's an old story."

"There is nothing that warms a girl's heart like the smile on the face of a sadist."

"And then he made promises: they wouldn't have to work. They'd be goddesses in the New Order simply by having children, simply by being able to give birth. No sweat, you know."

"He'd put their husbands to work, save their sons from crime. Big Daddy."

"So they voted for him. They married him. And right after the wedding, he started to slap them around."

"The laws?"

"The laws." The lobby was like a steam bath. Eve wiped her brow. She really felt sick. Maybe she would leave. "Now, I imagine at first the laws seemed okay. Racial science was well known throughout the world, and scientists were split on it. We had it here, you know, the brain of a Negro weighs less. Women's brains are smaller. And they trusted it. They trusted him.

The laws ensured their goddessdom, he told them. The laws protected them. And I'm sure they never thought the laws could apply to them. Until they realized power wasn't theirs just for reproducing. They had to reproduce perfectly."

"They'd married a control freak."

"Exactly. And they were trapped. Pregnant, if you will, and trapped. He booted them out of their jobs. Outlawed birth control. Made abortion a treasonable offense except in the case of "worthless life," where it was almost forcible. Sterilized them if they misproduced. Murdered them if they broke down."

"Broken promises?"

"False promises. He paid them to marry like he said he would, but they couldn't marry without proof of "racial soundness." He paid them to have children, but they were never allowed to stop. He purloined the children they had for Hitler Youth and Nazified them. And, if they didn't marry and have children, he took away their citizenship. As if that weren't enough, he sent their husbands and sons to war and put the women back to work in factories on double shift for slave wages."

"So they were like battered wives? That's why the women stuck to him?"

"I think so. There are still women in Germany saying the Führer couldn't have known. Babe, Adolf Hitler had his hands in the underpants of every German woman."

"There's an image. Are you okay?"

Eve was beginning to list.

"Yes. It's so hot in here. Are you hot?"

"Stifling. So is that it?"

"Almost. I'm still not sure how he got them to dump Christ for him."

"So they were trapped in a death marriage, no restraining orders there."

"No."

"Is it hard being a woman or what?" Babe asked. "See, you got off easy. What's a mushroom princess next to—hi, Charles." 139

Charles César was suddenly standing next to them.

" 'Allo, Babe," he said. " 'Allo, Eve."

Eve's heart was pounding. She could hardly breathe.

"Hi, I hope you don't mind," she began. "I just couldn't miss—is the projectionist okay?"

Her voice sounded false to her. She forced herself to look in his eyes, but he was looking away, down at her left arm, down at her buttoned sleeve.

"Yes, he's okay, poor man."

She felt herself perspiring. Maybe he didn't love her anymore. Maybe he didn't care.

"We will begin any minute now," he said and then, unable to stop himself, he asked, " 'Ow are you?"

"F-f-fine. Writing. Mingus had flu."

She was stuttering now.

"Who?" he asked, looking past her, surveying the lobby.

"Mingus. The cat."

Eve glanced at Babe. Eve was angry now.

"Ah, yes. Of course. The animal."

It was incredibly hot in the lobby. People were pressing against each other and sweating profusely. As time had passed, everyone had gotten drunk and their voices were loud and giddy. Charles César was jumpy. Eve felt sicker.

"It's a star-studded crowd, Charlie," Babe offered. "I see the Wesel brothers are here. Aren't they doing a film on teenage crack addicts?"

"Anything to get a date," Eve managed.

"And that guy who did the film on G.M. He looks exactly like he did on the "Today" show. Did you think he was anti-Semitic, Charlie? I didn't. At least no more so than most of America."

Babe was being heroic with the conversation. Eve and Charlie were just standing there opposite each other, soft-edged like butter sculptures. Eve's vision was blurring.

Louise Kowalski elbowed her way through the crowd, grabbed Charlie's arm proprietarily, and smiled. Charlie blushed.

140 Babe glanced at Eve. Eve stepped back and bumped into Stans-

field Hunt, millionaire backer playboy, who drunkenly quipped, "Ah, it's foul-penned little Evie. You look adorable tonight."

"Thank you and fuck you," Eve mumbled.

Babe laughed. Charles César and Louise looked upset.

"Excuse her Polish," Babe said to Louise.

Charlie wiped his brow.

"Eve," he said matter-of-factly, "this is Louise Kowalski. She has just finished a film on how pollution is destroying the medieval city of Krakow. Louise, this is Eve."

"How do you do?" mumbled Eve.

Eve was feeling most unsteady now. This Louise was younger than she looked across the lobby, maybe around thirty. She had a flat, Slavic face, luxuriant black hair, and the stony, self-possessed gaze of the Communist woman. Her tortoiseshell glasses softened this somewhat and gave her the aura of a Third World preppie. Jewish, Eve whispered to Eva, Jewish. She looks Jewish. She pictured Charlie fucking her.

"Pollution in Krakow," Babe was doing yeoman service. Eve would remember this. "That's a worthy subject."

"Yah," Louise replied. She has a strident voice. Doesn't she have a strident voice? "Your president has given us much money to save the city."

Eve looked at Charlie. What was it about him that had changed? He was the same man, the same guy she loved, and yet. She tried to imagine him as a Vatican cardinal, as she'd done so many times, but something was wrong, what was it? She put her hand on Babe's shoulder. She felt awful.

"One of his first priorities," Babe was saying. "He cares so damn much."

"Krakow? Isn't that near Auschwitz?" Eve heard herself say. But, before Louise could reply, Charlie said, "Louise, could you get me a drink."

And Louise nodded obediently and pushed off into the crowd.

Eve was face to face with Charlie. He was staring at her angrily, like she was something foreign to him, something distasteful. She stared back. What was wrong? What was it? She 141 tried picturing him as a Vatican cardinal in his cassock and zucchetto but it wasn't working. Why? Why? And then she knew. The zucchetto no longer looked like a cardinal's skullcap, it looked like a yarmulke. And he no longer looked like Charlie, the priest. He looked Jewish.

"Why did you come here?" He was furious.

"Charlie's Jewish," Eve turned to Babe. "Did you know that?"

Babe looked at Charlie curiously. His teeth were clenched so tight, his mouth appeared to be made of metal. The room was closing in on Eve. She had now done something irreparable. She held on to Babe's shoulder.

"I thought you were Catholic," Babe said. "You wear a crucifix around your neck. Is that a fashion statement?"

Charlie César fled into the crowd.

Eve fainted.

Babe screamed and leapt to her aid.

"Give her air!" Babe shouted.

And the throng waved back like an amoeba that had been poked. A moan of concern rippled through them. Human tragedy had struck the room. They wished they had their cameras.

"Get back!" Babe shouted.

She unbuttoned Eve's collar and cuffs and pushed up her sleeves. She fanned her with the playbill for Charlie's film and blew in her mouth. Some grips from public television offered their help as did a little old man with a heavy Eastern European accent.

"Is there a room we can get her to?" the old man asked.

The manager of the movie house beckoned and led the way. The grips hoisted Eve up. When he passed Charlie César, who was staring, transfixed by the scene, the manager whispered to him.

"We are ready now," Charlie announced robotically. "Please enter the theater."

The crowd swerved to the right. Eve came to.

"Go on, Babe," she said. "I'm fine. Go watch the film. I'll leave when I'm ready."

"Are you sure?" asked Babe.

"I've got her," the old man said. "Go."

And reluctantly, Babe went, promising, "I'll be back to check on you."

"Vat vas dat on her arm?" Louise Kowalski asked Babe as they pushed into the theater.

"Her Social Security number, dear," Babe told her. "We can all get them there if we want to. In a democracy, that's one of our options."

Eve looked up at the old man wiping her brow and smiled.

"Thank you," she murmured. "I don't know why—I met my boyfriend's new girlfriend and—"

"The pain of love. That could do it."

The old man smiled back. His face was a map of lines. His skin was parchment thin but his eyes were azure blue and shone with light. He was very graceful, almost effeminate in the way he moved, like a goblin or sprite.

The theater manager brought in a bowl of ice and a cloth and set them down. He was annoyed.

"I've caused some problems," Eve said sadly.

"Accch," the old man waved away her guilt.

He took off his suit coat, rolled up his shirtsleeves, and made a neat packet of ice in the washcloth. He sat down on the couch where she lay and placed the ice pack on her forehead. As his arm passed over her face, she saw the six little numbers tattooed on it.

Instantly she pulled down her sleeve.

"Too late. I've seen it," the old man said.

Eve burst into tears.

The old man pushed the ice pack down on her skin. It felt good.

"That's good. Relax. I won't bite," he said.

With his free hand, he picked up her arm and examined the tattoo. He rubbed it with his finger to see if it would come off.

"Hmmm," he muttered when he saw it was permanent.

Eve was ashamed. She closed her eyes and sobbed.

"So," he continued after a few moments, "you came to the kemp in 'forty-four about when Primo Levi came. Late in de war. Perhaps that's how you survived."

He was making a joke. Eve raised her eyes to him.

"How do you know?" she asked.

"It's a very high number. Mine is lower. I came in 'forty-three. You came from Germany. Late, though, very late. Unusual."

"Really?"

"Yah. Don't you know?"

"No. I know it's a woman's number. I saw her in a photograph. One day I'll find out about her."

"Ah."

"I'm wearing it like an MIA bracelet, you know, like we had in the Vietnam War?"

She forced herself to look in his eyes. They were twinkling and betrayed no judgment. She went on, "I call her Eva."

She stroked the tattoo.

"She will have life as long as I do. I tell people about her. I'm telling the histories of women who resisted and women who didn't and why."

"Why?" he asked.

"Why?" she repeated. "So many reasons."

She sagged back and shut her eyes. Her eyes were swelling, soaked with tears, but she said, "I'm a middle-class white American, a victim of unending privilege. I have life to spare."

"That's why I came here."

She opened her eyes. The old man was grinning.

"You needed a rest. Everyone who came here needed a rest. I was born here. I've rested enough."

The old man pressed the ice pack against her eyes. "How do you feel?" he asked.

"Ashamed," she replied, "to talk to you. You experienced it. I'm humbled in your presence."

The old man snorted cynically. "It wasn't my doing. If I could give it back, I would, believe me. I meant, how do you feel from the fainting?"

"Oh. That. Fine. Better. Thank you."

The old man placed the ice pack back in the bowl. He sat back, crossing his legs, posing his hands delicately on his knees, and appraised her. "You're not a Jew." He stated this.

"No. I'm a Christian, a WASP, the enemy. I'm an anti-Semite."

"Are you?"

"Yesterday I would have said no. But now, I—I realize I—"

Tears poured out of her eyes.

"Don't worry, for God's sake." The old man came over and sat her upright on the couch. "All Christians are anti-Semites."

She stared at him, surprised.

"They are? Do you really believe that?"

"That's my observation."

"Myself," he said, "I'm an anti-Hamite."

"An anti-Hamite?" Eve repeated.

"From Ham, the man who fathered the first tribe of Christians. An anti-Hamite. I hate Christians."

He was being facetious and yet, not.

"Because of the Nazis. Because of Auschwitz?" Eve asked.

"I've been forty-five years out of the camps, my dear. I've had other experiences with Christians."

"But your experience with the Nazis?"

"I wouldn't be what I am without it."

His eyes gleamed when he said this. He looked impish. There was no malice, no rancor in his tone. Eve was confused.

"Why do you hate Christians?" she asked.

She couldn't stop crying. She opened her purse and removed her handkerchief.

"What you believe. Stupid! Heaven, a stupid concept. A virgin gives birth. Goyim will swallow anything."

145

Eve took offense at this. "I hate that you don't believe in heaven and hell!" She was immediately ashamed that she'd said this to him.

"After the camps, I believe in hell," he said. "It's heaven I have trouble with."

"I can't talk to you about this. It isn't right."

A survivor. Why did she have to meet a survivor?

"You're so feminine. I wish to study you. Talk. Go on." He urged her with his gestures.

"We believe in resurrection out of this life. You believe this life is all there is or ever will be."

"Yah, opposing views. Goyim are stupid," he said again. "I love your arms, so long and slender. Wave for me, would you?"

Eve contemplated him. She waved one arm, the arm without the tattoo. "Jews are whiny and selfish," she said, waving it.

He looked at her, shocked.

"Prejudice," she added, "begins in ideology. Then it filters down into stereotypes."

That's it, she said to herself. That's how it began. The conversation about the afterlife with Charles César. She hung her head.

"Yah. You said something smart. So, what's wrong?"

"I found out my boyfriend was Jewish. I thought he was Catholic. He didn't want me to tell anyone. I betrayed him." Eve sobbed into her handkerchief.

The old man patted her on the back.

"This is biblical," he said.

"I hate myself so much. Who am I? What am I doing?" She wept bitterly.

"This is a good sign." He smiled at her.

"He'll never forgive me." She choked on her tears.

The old man pounded her.

"Relax, for God's sake. Women are all powerful. You have no idea. Your neck. The way you bend your neck when you cry— like a big flower stalk."

146   "You can take away a woman's power. Hitler did that. He

gave women medals for motherhood but he made it illegal to mother. In the end they were utterly powerless. They had given away themselves. All they had left was him."

The old man leaned toward her. He was more goblinesque than ever. His sexuality was indeterminate. He could have been a woman.

"Yah, your study of the women," he said.

"He got them to dump Christ for him. I don't know how he did that. I'm thinking about it."

"Is this a big deal?" he asked.

"Oh, sure." Eve blew her nose in her handkerchief. "Christian women? You bet. For me it would be. It's a sin. The ultimate sin. Like loving the devil." She burst into tears. "I did that. I just did that."

"Listen, listen." He took her hands. "You're such a shiksa. You believe so much. It's an anachronism."

"It's never failed me," she said, weeping, "until now. Do you think I could have been a Nazi?"

She stared into his eyes, waiting for his answer.

"You look so sincere. Stop it!" He laughed. "Your arms could belong to another woman, you know this? Look, only you can answer such a question. What made you do it just now?"

"Sex. But it wasn't for all time. They did it for good, the women."

"Perhaps it was something in the German character. An obscene reverence for nationalism?" He offered this.

"That can change, though. Look at us. In forty years we've gone from war hero to berserk vet. No, I don't believe that."

Forty years, she thought, there it was again, an eruptive time.

"How can the Israelis sell arms to South Africa? How can they corral the Arabs in camps? How?"

The old man looked sad for a moment. "I don't know," he answered. "I'm a Ben-Gurion Jew. Never forget—somebody forgot."

"Fundamentalism?" she asked.

"Fundamentalism," he agreed. Then he changed the subject. 147

"It interests me what you say about the women," the old man said. "Do you know about the Lebensborn program?"

Eve regarded him through swollen eyes.

"A little," she replied. "You mean the mating centers? Racially pure unmarried women mated with racially pure SS men to produce the super race. Another secret program. The one way an unmarried girl could get ahead. You mean that?"

"Yah," he said. "But there was another part to it. The Nazis kidnapped blond, blue-eyed children in the occupied countries and took them home to the Reich to raise them as Nazis. I was one of those children. They didn't know I'd turn into an old Jew."

He cackled mischievously.

"I want to tell you about it," he said.

"Please," she replied, drying her tears.

"I was born in Warsaw, Poland, in 1932. Yah, you're surprised. I look like an old man. That's my liver. It didn't recover from Auschwitz. Some did. Mine didn't. So what? Anyway. When the Nazis marched into Poland in 'thirty-nine, they started with the persecutions and my father was arrested on the street and shot. So then there was only my mother, who was twenty-seven, and me. One day I was in the street and some boys grabbed me and pulled down my pants to see if I was circumsized, if I was a Jew. And when they saw I was, they beat me up."

I told my mother, he went on, and that evening she came into my room with a box. "Here," she said, setting it on my bed. "Here are the tools of your survival."

I opened the box and inside was a little girl's party dress, party shoes and socks, and a little blond long-haired wig.

"The wig is only till your hair grows long," my mother said. "From now on, you will be a girl. It's safer."

Well, I cried. I screamed. I threw a tantrum. But my mother was adamant.

"You don't come out of your room until you're wearing the

dress," she said. "I will wait." She walked toward the door and then turned. "This is war, Jacob," she added, "not a game."

I stayed in my room for a day, staring at the dress. It was pink, very pretty, with embroidered flowers and a white lace collar. Late at night, I stood before the mirror and held it up in front of me. I could hear my friends laughing. I could hear their taunts.

The next day my mother came into my room. "We're leaving here tonight," she said. "We're becoming Aryans. I got a job as a maid for a Gentile. I"—she looked at herself in the mirror—"will be posing as an Aryan woman. You will be posing as an Aryan girl. We will both be posing. Like spies, you know, Jacob? You like spies."

That evening, my mother appeared and made me put on the dress. At first I struggled and I kicked her, and she threw herself on the bed crying.

"What do you want me to do? Leave you for the Nazis?" she cried.

I was ashamed of myself. So I slowly put on the dress and then the socks and party shoes and finally, the wig.

"Look, Mama," I said and touched her arm. She turned and looked and, with tears streaming down her face, she laughed out loud. Then she jumped up and pushed me toward the mirror.

"See, Jacob"—she laughed—"what a good disguise! Like a little Aryan girl. It's amazing!"

I have to say I was charmed. I was very pretty and, just like Mama said, as Aryan as any of the little girls I had seen on posters of the perfect family that the Nazis had pasted up around the city.

"None of your friends will know you. I'm sure of that," she added as she got our suitcases and headed for the door. I prayed that she was right.

As it happened, we ran into my best friend, Joseph, at the edge of the Jewish quarter. I don't know what he was doing there, something illegal, because when he saw my mother, he froze, looking very guilty. For her part, my mother had just removed her yellow star and had tossed it to the ground, and so, she, too, froze.

"Hello, Mrs. Markus," he stammered.

"Hello, Joseph," she replied.

Then they were both silent and embarrassed.

"Joseph," she said finally, "I haven't seen you and you haven't seen us. Understand?"

Joseph nodded and then he looked from her to me and his eyes widened with recognition. But instead of laughing, he seemed to get angry.

"The hell with you, Jacob," he cried and he turned and ran off back into the quarter.

For two years we lived with the Gentile family on the opposite side of Warsaw and my life was completely transformed. There were two little girls in the house and a boy my own age whom I longed to play with. I wanted to run fast and throw rocks and be a boy with him but I could not. I had to play with the little girls, endless tea parties and shopping with dolls. Once we played boycotting the Jewish tailor and I was the tailor's wife. I imitated a Mrs. Schwartz from the quarter and the girls screamed with laughter.

"Oooo, you're so good, Helga," Verna said to me. "You'll grow up to be an actress!"

My hair was long now and buttermilk blond. My eyes, the blue you see. You must take it for truth when I tell you that I was the most perfect Aryan specimen, like you. I studied the girls' movements and practiced them in my room.

Here the old man paused and stood up. Bending his head in a coquettish, feminine manner, he tiptoed across the floor and became a female child. Eve applauded.

"That's uncanny," she said smiling.

The old man bowed, sat down again, and resumed.

*   *   *

Yah, I was an expert. In my mind, however, I became crazy. As I couldn't be a boy, I began to become a girl. I began to think that God had simply made a mistake and the energy I stifled burst out into little rages during which I destroyed animals. A cat, birds, dogs. I don't like to think of it now.

I was so lovely and delicate that our neighbor, a woman who owned a department store that had been taken from Jews, asked my mother if I could be in a fashion show she was having for some Nazi wives and their friends. My mother refused, of course, but the neighbor persisted, and I wanted to do it. I had grown proud of my beauty and Verna and Magda egged me on, lauding my abilities.

"She's just like Shirley Temple," they told the neighbor. "Please make her mother say yes."

Finally, to avoid suspicion, my mother gave in.

"I don't like this, Jacob," she said. "I'm afraid."

"Mama," I told her, "I'm so good. Even you think so. What can happen?"

"Who's going to change your clothes, boy?" she asked, glancing significantly at my groin.

"You, Mama," I said. "And we wrap it flat."

My mother looked at me and sighed. "I curse you, Adolf Hitler," she muttered, and nodded her head in assent.

The week of the show, my mother got ill, very ill. She could not rise from the bed. She did manage, however, to wrap up my genitals. Round and round my hips she wound the cloth, and fastened it with a pin.

"Dress yourself," she whispered. "And if anyone sees this bandage under your camisole, say you have a hernia. Do you understand? A hernia."

The store was ablaze with lights when we arrived there. The Nazi wives were arranged like flowerpots on little spindly-legged chairs. They were dressed in furs and jewels and lovely dresses and velvet gloves. Their hair was coiffed and shiny, and they wore makeup and red lips, which shocked us little girls, for we'd been told the perfect woman wears no paint and is at one with nature. Also, they were drinking champagne out of crystal, fluted glasses. Drinking liquor! And laughing! So much cheerful laughing! We weren't used to this at all. The women we knew rarely laughed anymore; they were always worried.

Behind the stage, I received my outfits and was told to dress with the other girls in a large, communal dressing room.

"Pardon, ma'am," I beseeched the lady in charge of us, "I cannot dress with the others. I am too modest."

"Little brat," she mumbled to herself. But because I was the star of the show, she brought me a screen, behind which I dressed.

Oh, it was exciting and fun. These lovely violins played around me as I strolled down the runway in a little woolen coat with matching hat and leggings and fur muff. In my mind, I metamorphosed in that moment. I became, for sure, a girl. Shirley Temple. Sonja Henie. I was them. I was a hit. The Nazi wives loved me. They cuddled and kissed me and stroked my golden hair.

"It's hard to believe she's Polish," I heard one say.

The neighbor who brought me was delayed going home. She asked another woman to watch me until she was ready to leave, but I was so full of my own success, it seemed to me I might walk home alone. I knew the way, and after all, I was a star. I asked permission to go to the bathroom and left the building.

A block from the store, some SS were standing by the line of cars belonging to the Nazi wives. They were talking with the chauffeurs. They saw me and began whispering to each other. As I passed by, they grabbed me, putting their hands over my mouth, and dragged me into a car. Then I was driven off. I struggled. Then something was placed on my nose, and I passed out.

I woke up in a large room filled with children, all sitting or standing on little wooden beds. Some were crying. Most were glum. All were blond and blue-eyed like me. There was a beautiful boy of about eight, slumped on the bed next to mine. I spoke to him.

"Are we going to die?" I asked, for my mother had impressed upon me that since I was Polish and Jewish, death would come for me if I were caught.

"I don't know," he answered. "They say we are going to Germany to live."

"To work in factories?" I asked. "Aren't we very small?"

I knew about the deportation of labor from the cook in the Gentile's house. She often talked of it. Her sister was in Hamburg, working in a ball-bearings plant.

"Not work," he replied sadly. "I don't think it's work."

At this moment, a German woman in a Nazi uniform entered the room and made an announcement.

"*Kinder,* listen here," she began. "We have contacted your parents and they send you their love." The room quieted when she said this. Perhaps our parents were coming to get us. We listened carefully.

"Your parents agree with us that you will be safer in Germany, safe from the bombings and fighting, and the Jews. You are such racially eugenic children, exemplary specimens, that your parents have begged us to place you with new families in the Fatherland, where you will thrive and grow strong."

"She didn't speak to my mother," I whispered to the beautiful boy.

"My mother's dead," he responded mournfully. "But maybe my grandmother said it was all right. She doesn't like me."

The Nazi woman went on.

"Please line up—girls on one side, boys on the other, and we have baths and clean clothes and prepare for the trip. *Kommt!*"

I was terrified. A bath would be my undoing. They would see I was not a girl, but a boy and a Jew, and then they would kill me. I thought of my mother and how she said, "Jacob, I'm afraid." I began to cry.

"*Kommt!*" the Nazi woman called to me but I did not move.

She walked over to me and raised up my chin with her hand, peering into my eyes. "What's the matter?" she asked.

"I have a hernia," I said sweetly. "I'm not allowed to bathe. I must wash at the sink with a cloth."

She frowned and thought to herself for a moment.

"Let me see," she commanded.

I pulled up my dress and camisole, and showed her the bandage.

"All right. Stay here," she barked. "I will see about this."

And she marched the other children out of the room. About twenty minutes later, she returned with an SS man.

"Ach, it's a shame," he said when he saw me. "Lovely child. But she's a Pole after all. Genetically weak."

"What shall we do with her?" the woman asked.

"We throw her back. Only racially eugenic children for the Lebensborn program. No defects."

"But no one is to know." The woman stared at him.

"I myself," he sighed, "am not in the business of killing children. My orders are to pick out the best ones and bring them back to the Fatherland. *Kom,* little girl," he addressed me, "I will throw you back into the sea where I netted you. God help you."

And taking me by the hand, he led me to a car and drove me back to the department store where he found me.

"So you were saved?" Eve asked.

"That time, yes. Two years later, though, someone denounced my mother and me to the Gestapo and we were deported to Auschwitz."

"You went as a girl?"

"Yah, until we were on the train and a boy my age died. My mother suddenly removed a scissors from a hidden pocket in her hem and cut off my hair. She stole the clothes of the dead boy and made me put them on. Of course I fought her. I would have stayed a girl forever by that time, but she swore to me that being a boy was my only hope of survival. She was correct. All the little girls in our transport were gassed immediately. My best performance of all was as a strapping youth, capable of work, on the selection ramp. My mother survived as well. Ours is a happy ending."

"Thank God," said Eve.

"Oh, I forgot," he added, grinning, "they did measure my skull. Perfect example of the Aryan female."

"More science based on looks," said Eve, mostly to herself.

The old man stood up and put on his suit coat. He took Eve's hand and kissed it, and, bowing to her, made for the door. The way he was walking, the way he moved his arms, Eve had the distinct impression that he was imitating her.

"Sir," she called to him.

He stopped and turned.

"When Christianity works, it's about love. What's Judaism about when it works?"

"I don't wish to tell you," he said, smiling. "That's another difference between us."

Babe flung open the door and burst into the room. "Are you okay?" she asked.

"Fine," Eve replied.

Babe looked at the old man.

"Hello, Mr. Schlaren," she said respectfully.

"Hello," he said to Babe and then to Eve, "Good-bye. I shall ponder your arms."

And he disappeared through the door.

"Isn't he wonderful?" exclaimed Babe. "Didn't you love him? Jacob Schlaren, the great Yiddish transvestite. He's renowned in Yiddish theater. I saw his act in France once. Unreal. He's exactly like a woman. Odd profession for a survivor of the camps, isn't it?"

XIX

It was the day Eve had chosen to find out the identity of 500123, the prisoner she called "Eva." She had made an appointment at YIVO, the Yiddish Scientific Institute, for 11 a.m. that morning but, because the boiler in her building had broken down, she was running late.

The thermometer outside her window read fifteen degrees. It was gray and overcast, threatening to snow. Inside, her apartment was stone cold and silent. No reassuring whistles and hisses emanated from the radiators. There was just this hard iciness in the air that, combined with the lack of hot water, set her nerves on edge and her muscles to spasm. She moved crankily around her apartment in her topcoat, hunched over like an old woman.

As she dialed the superintendent, her mind drifted to accounts she'd read of Auschwitz prisoners in winter. No coats. No shoes. No windows in the barracks. Minimal food and water. And through it all, working at hard labor, sick and starving, broken and forgotten. She thought of Mr. Schlaren. She did not know how he had survived it. She couldn't even imagine. "Mussulmen," "Moslems," they called the ones who gave up and staggered around, living dead, until they actually died. That would have been herself. "Was that you, Eva?" she wondered out loud. Today, perhaps, at YIVO, she would find out.

The superintendent came on the line.

"How's it going, Mr. Juarez?" This was their third conversation of the morning.

"They say they be here at noon, Evie."

"You believe them?"

"How I know?"

"Okay. All right. Don't be afraid to be firm. The firmest people get preference in New York. This isn't the islands."

"Yes. I do my best."

"That's all anyone can do. Call you later."

She put down the phone and stared at it for a long time. She had to call Charles César. What will I say to him? she asked Eva. What can I say?

"Darling," she was speaking out loud. Her lips trembled from cold and anxiety. "Please forgive me. Please, please, I—"

She dialed his number. She had gotten it from Cilla. He was subletting down in Soho, someplace. She hadn't spoken to him since the night of the betrayal, three days ago.

"Forgive me for I have sinned."

The phone was ringing. Her heart was skipping. Her lips were shaking like Jell-O.

"I realize I—"

"Hallo?"

The phone was answered by a woman, a Polish accent, Louise Kowalski.

Eve was so flustered she could hardly talk. Maybe she should hang up. Was he living with this woman? Why had no one warned her?

"Hallo?" Louise said again.

"May I speak to Charles César, please?"

Eve's anger was erupting. She could hear it in her tone.

"Who's calling, please?" Louise asked.

"Eve," she said and then added, "Eve Flick."

"Hold on." Louise put down the phone and walked someplace. She could hear her. Charlie. Charlie. Please forgive me, please.

"Eve?"

It was her again. What was going on here?

"He doesn't want to talk to you," Louise said gleefully, and hung up.

Eve hurt so much she blacked out on what happened next. She thought she went out of her mind. When she came back, she dimly recalled hurling herself around the room, sobbing and screaming until Mingus burrowed under the bedclothes and would not come out. When, finally, she had hold of herself, she sat down gently on the bed and said to him, "I'm going to see about Eva, Ming."

The covered lump shivered in recognition.

"That's the most important thing. More important than all the Louises in Communist-free Poland."

Stiff with defiance, Eve ducked into the stationery store to buy a paper. She stood there, trying to read it, trying to focus amid waves of sorrow.

The Europeans were getting anxious, she read. Now that the champagne had been consumed, their terrors were surfacing. Poland was concerned about its border. They feared the Germans would take back the strip of land ceded to them after the war. They feared the Germans would march again. There were interviews with Englishmen who had fought the Nazis and were dubious at best. Suddenly the Soviets were mentioning their millions who had died.

She was out of step with her countrymen, she thought. How Americans loved a party! Unhampered by history, starved for delight, they remained exhilarated by the German festivities, more or less convinced that Nazism was a concept that surfaced every few years in Hollywood. People in chaos, she thought, perceive control as freedom.

"How's Charlie?"

Walter, the very nice guy who ran the stationery store, was talking to her over the counter.

"Oh. Fine. Fine." She managed a smile. There was that pain in the pit of her stomach.

"Uh, I think you owe me." Walter was smiling at her questioningly.

She was standing with her hand out waiting for change.

"I'm sorry," she said and paid him for the paper.

"Say hi to Charlie," he called as she drifted out of the store.

As she waited on the corner, hailing a cab, an icy wind blew up her skirt and froze her thighs. He'll never forgive me, Eva. I betrayed him and I'm an anti-Semite. I'm not worthy of the tattoo. I'm not worthy of you.

"Eve!"

Eve dragged herself out of her mind to see Harry Allbright, a real-estate millionaire, who had lately been pursuing her. She didn't want to see him now. She didn't want to speak to him.

"Hello, Harry," she replied.

Harry was a good-looking man in his fifties who wanted her for his mistress. He was extremely rich and, as Scott Fitzgerald had put it, different. Perhaps, she thought as he approached, this was because he had spent his youth making money, parlaying intangibles. There seemed to be no depth to him at all. Once, at an outdoor café, he had refused a dollar to a homeless beggar on the grounds it would spoil the man for work. He hung a poster of the '72 Olympics in the room he kept for his six-year-old son. When she pointed out to him that that was the Olympics at which the Israeli team was slaughtered, he replied that the poster was pretty.

See, Eve, you're not a Nazi. It isn't quite that simple.

"Hi, Pumpkin," Harry said.

Eve gestured nervously with the newspaper.

"It's good the Europeans are thinking about it. Did you see? It's terribly important to think about it and talk about it. So many people died."

"C'mon, Evie," Harry laughed condescendingly. He was angry at her for not sleeping with him. "It's all about money. It has nothing to do with morals. Trust me."

I hated Charlie for being Jewish. I hated him, Eva.

"Lunch?" Harry was asking.

And Charlie felt the hatred. He felt it.

"No, Harry. I can't. I need a cab." Tears were filling her eyes.

The person who destroys you is the person who helps you the most. Relationship therapy, Eve.

Tell it to Germany.

"Allow me," Harry was saying. He went into the street to get her a cab.

Eve stepped off the curb and stood in front of a parked van, waiting.

What am I doing? I thought I was pure. I thought I was clean.

"All my friends are dating women in their twenties, Eve," Harry was shouting to her, "you should write about it."

She was going to reply but she never got the chance. The parked van lurched forward and hit her. The next thing she knew, she was spread-eagled on the ground with the van wheel rolling over her back. As it thumped across her stomach, she threw up, and time stopped.

"Oh, my God," Harry had just seen her. She watched with detachment as he shouted and ran toward her. Then she was above her body, looking down, surveying the scene. She was hovering there, watching herself throw up. Penance came to her mind, penance. And then she flipped over and was lying on a table cradled in white, soothing light, and a male voice was comforting her. "You'll be all right," he said, "don't worry. You'll be all right."

And then she was back in her body. The second van wheel was coming. She awaited it calmly. It rolled over her back, thumping her to the ground, and she relaxed, believing, sighing with its weight. And then it was over and she lay on the ground, torn and bruised, her cheek ice cold against the avenue.

The homeless man from the pocket park sat down by her side and began stroking her forehead.

"Praise God," he shouted. "Praise Him!"

"Are you all right? Oh, my God, are you all right?"

Harry was shaking.

"Yes. What happened? I think my arms are broken."

She looked down at her arms. She had fallen on them. One, the one with the tattoo, the one with Eva, was bleeding.

"A guy hit the van from behind. Drunk. Trying to park. Don't worry. I'll be back."

Walter rushed over now and held her hand.

"The ambulance is on the way," he said. "Shall I call Charlie?"

XX

The ambulance arrived and carted Eve off to Mother Cabrini, a Catholic hospital in the East Twenties. Harry had offered to come but she refused him. She had to be alone. She had to contemplate what had happened to her.

When she was carried into the hospital, the first thing she saw was a huge Jesus Christ on a cross. Hanging there sad and tortured, on the emergency-room wall, he gave her a sinking feeling. Perhaps she was going to die. Perhaps the voice had been misinformed. She began trembling. Shock, she told herself, just shock. And, of course, she'd lain on the freezing ground for quite a while before the ambulance came.

Two nuns, nurses in white habits, approached with scissors. They were going to cut her clothes off. She looked down and became aware of her state of disarray. No shoes. Her coat torn and filthy, and across its white wool, tire marks, treads and all, like a good Xerox on white paper.

She touched her face and found that her forehead was swollen like a grapefruit. Her upper lip felt odd, swollen too. She tasted blood. Her left arm was beginning to throb. From the depths of her consciousness, pain was beginning to surface. She couldn't move it. Well, she thought, well.

The nuns set about cutting her clothes. In two pieces the coat. In four, the dress. And each time they eased her out of a sleeve, this increasing pain.

162

"Is it broken?" she asked.

"I think so, dear," Sister Mary said.

"Oh, yes," Sister Elizabeth agreed.

In one swoop, they peeled off her panty hose and left her in her bra and pants. She examined herself as best she could. Bruises surfacing everywhere. The right forearm was sprouting a goose egg. The left was a bloody mass. The tattoo was invisible, crusted with blood. Eva? Eva? Are you all right? Oh, my God, Eva.

The nuns returned and helped her into an angel robe.

"It will be a while, dear. Try and calm yourself," Sister Mary said and vanished beyond the curtain.

No. He said I'd be all right, Eve thought. I'm American. I'm white. I've got insurance. I've got it made. Nothing can harm me except myself.

Auschwitz, she thought, what if this had happened at Auschwitz. She'd read that sometimes the Nazis took care of the wounded, fixed them up only to gas them. Sometimes they didn't. Just let wounds fester. It depended on your usefulness, what work they needed you for, whether you were worthless life. Eva, lying on some patch of Polish ground, arm mangled. Eva. She began to cry. Shock, she told herself, just shock. He said you'd be all right, but you don't deserve to be.

A doctor opened the curtain now and came into the cubicle. He was tall and funny-looking and gazed at her quizzically. "What happened?" he asked.

"I was run over by a truck," she replied. Her voice sounded faint to her.

"You look like it," the doctor said and smiled. "Let's see that arm."

He touched her left arm and she cried out inadvertently. The pain was so great it made her breathless.

He fingered it for a moment during which time she held her breath to keep from screaming. Gulps of moans escaped her despite her efforts.

"Okay," he said, placing her arm on the bed, leaving her in 163 flooding sweats of relief. "They'll be in to take you to X-ray, and then we have to operate. It's pretty shattered. How do you feel otherwise?"

"I'm all right," she said with conviction.

"All right. We'll see. We'll be looking for internal bleeding."

"Painkiller?" she managed.

He shook his head. "Not till after X-ray. Sorry." Good. It was good that she should suffer. Good that she should hurt. Penance.

Sister Mary and Sister Elizabeth reappeared and set about cleaning her wounds.

"Do I look awful?" she asked.

The sisters glanced at each other.

"The swellings will go down," Sister Mary said.

"Oh, yes, very soon," added Sister Elizabeth.

"Hang on, dear," said Sister Mary. "This is going to sting." And she picked up Eve's arm and began to bathe it.

Eve gasped and emitted little animal cries she had never heard issue from her mouth.

"Hmmm," Sister Mary made an inquiring sound that summoned Sister Elizabeth to her side. The sisters looked closely at Eve's forearm and then at each other.

"Is . . . something . . . wrong?" Eve got out.

"Are you a punk, dear?" Sister Elizabeth peered at her with surprise.

Eve tried to look where they were looking. It was at the tattoo. Still there, still visible but ragged, just at the edge where the skin was severed. Beneath it, white bone protruded. Eve dropped her head back so she wouldn't faint.

Sister Mary finished cleaning her arm and placed it on the bed. The pain receded again. As long as no one moved it, the arm throbbed but the intense pain was hidden behind the shock that surged to the fore now, pumping her full of adrenaline. She had to talk. She had to tell them about Eva.

"That tattoo," she said, "the number of a Catholic prisoner

who died at Auschwitz. Eva Hartz. I have to tell you about her in case I die. Please."

The nuns were tidying up the cleaning cloths. They stopped when she said this and leaned in to hear what she would say.

"When Eva Hartz was little, she wanted to be a nun," Eve began in a faint voice.

The nuns smiled.

"But when she grew up, she amended that. She felt she was too sinful. She decided instead to open a welfare center.

"In 1930," Eve told them, "she graduated from Catholic high school and went on to teachers' college. And two years later, with the help of the Jesuit fathers, she achieved her dream. She opened a storefront charity for poor and indigent Berliners. At the age of twenty-one, the youngest Catholic woman ever to do so."

Eve breathed deeply. Her strength was pulsating. She went on.

"Eva had counted on a simple life but, in 1933, when the Nazis came to power, she found herself in the midst of a confusion she would spend her youth trying to solve.

"You see, the Nazis turned out to be anti-Catholic."

The nuns looked at each other and shook their heads in disgust. They knew something of this.

This came as quite a shock to Eva, Eve continued. She knew Adolf Hitler had been raised Catholic, had even wanted to be an abbot. And so, she voted for him, assuming that, in his Germany, Catholics would be well treated, if not privileged. But in 1933, the Nazis arrested and murdered three thousand Catholic liberals including Father Heinz, her beloved mentor and confessor, and she realized she been duped.

She was barely over her grief about Father Heinz, when she was shocked again. She heard the pope had signed a Concordat with Hitler. The pope promised Catholics would support Hitler if the Nazis would defend and support Catholics. A copy of the Vatican Concordat arrived that summer at the center and Eva posted it on the wall of her office so she could meditate on it and understand why the church would overlook the murder of Father Heinz. Well, she thought, the Concordat would end Nazi hostility. Too late for Father Heinz, but not, perhaps, for others.

A copy of the Racial Hygiene directives from the Nazi government also arrived that summer and sent her around the bend. She went to Father Meerschaum, another of her teachers in the Catholic hierarchy, and sought his advice.

"Father," she began. It was embarrassing to have to discuss this with a man. She steeled herself. "It says here that I am to recommend forcible sterilizations, propagandize against unmarried, childless women, endorse unwed motherhood. These directives are contrary to our teachings. How am I to counsel motherhood outside the family? How can I deprive any woman of her right to bear children? Since when are spinsters unworthy of Christian love? And look at this—" She leaned over the huge, wooden desk and handed Father Meerschaum the paper. "My counseling is not to be religious but Nazified. Read there. It says children are to be educated and trained as Nazis, not Catholics. Father?"

Father Meerschaum sighed. He looked weary. "Do as your conscience tells you, Eva," he told her. "Do only what your conscience tells you."

She followed Father Meerschaum's advice. She ignored the directives and heeded her conscience, but in 1934, during the purge of Ernst Röhm and his S.A. brownshirts, Father Meerschaum was murdered, too. She began watching and waiting to see what would happen next.

As the directress of a charity in a poor, crowded neighborhood, Eva saw and heard many things. The Nazis came and hung their banners and flags alongside the saints in the Catholic churches. Mothers, forced to put their children in Hitler Youth and Frauenbund, deluged her with horror stories. They are teaching Hitler as Christ, they whispered. It is blasphemy.

Down the street from her charity was a health clinic that the Nazis constantly raided. The Catholic nurses there refused to perform sterilizations. The Catholic doctors, by virtue of their superior position, had wriggled out of it. They had been granted a reprieve by the state. That left the nurses, who refused. Eva cheered them on, giving them support and hiding places when they needed to disappear. But finally the Nazis closed the clinic down.

Eva herself received weekly visits from Frau Kurtz, head of the local chapter of the Nazi Women's League, checkups, really, to see if the charity was counseling Catholicism. Eva never backed down. As Frau Kurtz railed at her about obeisance to the Führer, the glory of the Reich, and the import of the purity of the Aryan race, Eva would lean back in her chair and point to the copy of the Concordat taped to the wall.

"God help you, Frau Kurtz," she cried out once, having lost control during one of the lectures. "You deny God! You deny Christ! Have you no fear?" And Frau Kurtz appeared shaken. But soon after, Eva was called in for questioning by the Ministry of Religious Affairs. She got off with a warning, but from then on her mail was opened, her telephone was tapped, and the center was watched. And Frau Kurtz got a promotion.

The Nazi concept of "worthless life" terrified Eva. It was directly contrary to what she saw as the basic tenets of her church—that all life was precious and worthy of love, including unborn life, idiot life, sickly life—all God's creatures. This concept of worthless life was so inimical to her, in fact, that any time she had to deal with it in the daily running of the charity, she vomited. Just like a child who eats meat on Friday. It went that deep. And so she went to discuss it again, this time with Father Bund, the priest who had replaced Father Heinz. She did not go to his office. She went to confess to him.

On her knees in the dark confessional, she poured out her heart. "Father," she said, "I am commanded by the state to commit mortal sins. I am to counsel abortion to indigent, sickly women, recommend them for sterilization without their knowledge. I cannot speak of God. Father, help me. What am I to do?"

Father Bund's voice was low and warm. "The pope has endorsed the Nazi state, my child, and it is glorious on Earth. Do as you are told. God is with them." Eva rose from her knees, crying. She walked out of the confessional, into the church festooned with Nazi flags, and returned to the charity. As far as her mission was concerned, she knew she was now on her own.

There were Jews in the neighborhood and Eva was kind to them. When, one by one, they were ejected from their employments and could no longer feed their children, she gave them food. When the workers at her charity complained, fearing reprisal, she told them, "We are all equal under God, Jews as well." And she stepped up her work, taking in Jewish men who had been beaten in the street, and bathing their wounds.

"You're riding for a fall, Fraulein Hartz," the MRA man warned her the fifth time she was summoned for interrogation. He had been two classes ahead of her at Catholic school.

"We'll see about that in heaven, Christian," she replied, calling him by his given name. He had the good sense to blush.

But Eva was in constant trouble now. The final blow was a new directive that prohibited sterilized persons from marrying, even other sterilized persons. Eva couldn't handle it.

"So," she shouted at the next meeting of her workers, "not only do we take a woman's right to bear children, we take her right to marry, and we take it without her knowledge!? Excuse me——" And she went and vomited in the W.C.

Once again she was called in for questioning.

"Here"—the MRA man handed the paper to her—"is the Catholic hierarchy's memo complying with the ban on marriage for sterilized persons. Here is the archbishop's advocation of divorce in cases of sterility." He handed her another paper.

"And here"—she handed him a paper of her own—"is the Vatican Concordat. I am a Catholic, Christian, and the Führer has sworn to protect me. Catholic. You know well what that means: no limiting of childbearing except abstinence, no divorce, no abortion. And what are these prayers the children learn in Hitler Youth: Führer, my Führer sent to me from God,

I thank thee for my daily bread? The Third Reich comes, thy will alone is law upon earth? THY will ALONE!? What happened to Christ's will? What happened to Christ?"

To which the MRA man replied with hanging head, "This must end badly, Eva. I am ordered."

In 1935, Nazi welfare officials banned all motherhood training programs not directed by the Nazi Women's Bureau, and Eva's charity was eviscerated and left to care only for bums and tramps. She soldiered on, providing the best care she could for the lost souls, and when, in that same year, the Nuremburg Laws were passed, she secretly increased her work with Jews. She provided what help she could for those in illegal mixed marriages. She did not counsel divorce, of course, but found homes in the country where Aryan partners could hide until Christ, in his mercy, saw fit to oust the political devil.

She continued her weekly visits to the Catholic home for wayward girls, which had yet to be shut down. Here she had many a pitched battle with Frau Jergen of the Nazi Women's Bureau, who had replaced the Catholic director.

"I will not counsel having children outside the family. I cannot!" Eva shouted when Frau Jergen reprimanded her for a lecture.

"The *volk* is our family now!" Frau Jergen shouted back. "Mothers and fathers are only the biological catalyst. Can't you see that?"

Eva felt nauseated. "No," she replied, "no, no, no." And then she excused herself to use the W.C.

At the beginning of 1937, the Nazis outlawed all religious institutions, including schools and charitable centers, and Eva's storefront was closed. She continued her clandestine work with the Jews, now finding hiding places for them in vacant apartments throughout the neighborhood. And she secretly taught Catholic children about Christ out of her home. She married that year after extracting a promise from her husband that he would not ejaculate inside her until the Nazis were ousted.

"We will be suspect," he protested.

But she was adamant.

"The Nazis will take our children," she said. "God will drive them out. We're young. We can wait."

In March of 1937, Pope Pius XI finally condemned Nazi racial policy. Eva was sent a copy of His Holiness's speech along with one by Cardinal Faulhaber denouncing the Nazis for breaking the Concordat. Now we'll see, she thought, the battle is on. But then she heard that Hitler had removed religious issues from the MRA and assigned them to the SS. She knew she was now in danger.

Eva was told she was on the SS list of those to watch and so she returned to work to cover her activities. As so many jobs were closed to women and Catholics, she became an orderly in a mental hospital outside of Berlin.

In the fall of 1939, when Germany invaded Poland, she was still working there. Her husband was called up and so she no longer worried about getting pregnant. Her husband had held to his word, but God had blessed them several times nonetheless. She was recovering from her second miscarriage when she began to notice sinister doings in the asylum where she worked. Children under three years of age began dying at an alarming and inexplicable rate.

One morning she entered Ward B to find six severely deformed babies stone dead in their cribs. She ran for Nurse Faust, and the two of them rushed back to the now strangely silent ward. The other six deformed little souls, still alive, wept with strangled cries and thrashed uncontrollably.

"It's as if they know something," whispered Eva.

Nurse Faust hugged herself with her arms. Nurse Faust was Catholic, too.

"What do they know?" demanded Eva.

"Five in Ward C yesterday. Four in A the day before. I've seen some death certificates: pneumonia, peritonitis, appendicitis."

"That can't be," Eva said.

Nurse Faust was white as a sheet.

"No," she agreed in a soft voice. "That can't be."

A week later, Eva arrived at the asylum to find the wards were cold as ice. Three babies had frozen to death in the night.

"Good God," she said to Nurse Faust. "The boiler broke down in the night and three babies have died!" She burst into tears.

Tears ran down Nurse Faust's face, but her voice was grim.

"No, Eva, it is policy now. No heat in the children's wards at night during winter."

Eva marched into the office of the asylum director Herr Doctor Bosch.

"Sir," she began, "three babies in Ward B have frozen in the night due to the lack of heat. I am told this is policy. Surely——"

Herr Doctor Bosch rose from his desk and put his arm around her shoulder. "Eva," he said, "there's a war on. Fuel is to be rationed all over the Reich. Our allotment is minuscule. I am doing the best I can."

Eva tried to look into his eyes but he glanced away.

"But surely, sir, the heat could be off during the day when we are here and can warm the children with coats and blankets, our bodies if necessary."

Herr Doctor looked surprised. He clearly had no answer for this.

"I have received directives. There is nothing I can do." He sighed heavily and began to escort her from the room.

"Perhaps I will volunteer then to come and warm them at night. Maybe others will come, too."

Now Herr Doctor fixed her with a stare. "For what, Eva? These are creatures who cannot stop shaking, who have no arms or legs or faces, or brains. No cerebellums, no frontal lobes, brains swollen with fluid. Skins too sensitive to touch. For what, Eva? Why?"

"Because they are alive, Herr Doctor. We do not keep them alive by artificial means. God keeps them alive. And they smile, Herr Doctor, and laugh when I hold them. Reichs-marschall Göring has outlawed vivisection of animals because it is cruel. Surely he has not condoned the murder of German children?"

Herr Doctor Bosch turned and went back to his desk. He said nothing. After a few moments, Eva went back to Ward B. She got together all the Catholic nurses and orderlies and proposed the warming plan. By unanimous vote, they agreed on it. That is how Eva came to be at the asylum the night of the first mass gassing of adult mental patients.

One night in January of 1940, Eva arrived at the asylum to find the SS parked outside. She was, of course, afraid, but not because of her work with the Jews. It was her warming plan. It had created a constant battle with asylum administrators. It had become clear to Eva that, though they refused to admit it, they were, in fact, through their withholding of heat, killing off the children, the "worthless life" of the directives she so despised. Other Catholic orderlies in other asylums confirmed her suspi-cions, reporting phenol injections, morphine, sleeping powders, and cyanide administered to the children. She had met with the other orderlies and they had a plan to go en masse to the archbishop, on the following Wednesday, and register an all-Catholic-worker protest. Perhaps, she worried as she entered the asylum, the SS had got wind of it.

The hospital was warm. The heat was on, probably for the SS, and as she walked past the director's office, she noticed that all the top doctors were present. Unusual. She hurried along the corridor to the back stairway up to the children's wards and, glancing out the window on the landing, saw something that shook her. Recently, two crematoria had been installed on the grounds, "to deal," as Herr Doctor Bosch told her, "with un-claimed dead. This is wartime, Eva. Shortage of workers." The crematoria were being stoked up. As if dead were expected. As far as she knew, bodies were cremated on Mondays and Fridays. This was Wednesday. It was night. Cremating was done during the day. Her heart began to flutter. She hurried upstairs into Ward B.

The ward was icy. A look at the radiators told her that they had been disconnected from their heating pipes. She shuddered with disgust.

The other orderlies who helped her were clustered by the window staring down at the smoking crematoria.

"There's something going on, Eva," Marlena whispered. "The east wing where they built the new showers is blocked off. Twenty special workers were admitted there about six this evening. The non-Catholic nursing staff is on extra duty there and not talking. Twenty patients from Adult Ward A were led in there about ten minutes ago."

"My brother's a plumber," Erna whispered. "He works here sometimes. He told me there's no water pipes leading to those showers. He was fixing toilets in the east wing last week. He says they are gas pipes."

"Oh God," Eva said. "Surely not. Surely not?!"

Eva fell to her knees before the cross of Jesus that hung on the wall near them.

"Oh, dear God, help us," she prayed aloud. One by one the other orderlies joined her on their knees, heads bowed. "Tell us what we can do to stop this evil. Oh, dear God." And she made the sign of the cross.

"Let us go in a group," she said, rising determined.

"The SS is here," Marlena said. They all looked at the floor.

"I've got to go," Eva said.

"We have the babies to think of," Erna said.

"I'll go with you," said Effie. "My brother's in the SS."

And Effie and Eva strode down the hall to the east wing.

It was indeed locked when they arrived, and in front of the double doors stood three SS men, one of whom, thankfully, Effie knew.

"Hi, Werner," she said cheerfully. "We need to get some catheters from the supply room. Can we pass?"

"No, Effie," he replied. He was uneasy. "In about five minutes, it will be over. Then."

"What, Werner? What's going on?" Effie was flirting. Eva smiled at the other two coquettishly.

Werner shook his head, and at that moment the double doors opened and five workers pushed through. They were unknown to Effie and Eva and they wore rubber gloves that were covered with blood, and they carried pliers. Their eyes were blank and their faces nauseated. They were followed by one of the head doctors, who was carrying a tray on which were strewn twenty or twenty-five tiny pieces of gold. Effie and Eva scurried away behind a pillar and watched as he rushed down the hall.

"What was he carrying? Did you see?" Effie whispered to Eva.

It took Eva a few moments to say it out loud.

"Tooth fillings," she finally replied.

"The Nazis arrested Eva on the Wednesday morning of the mass protest to the archbishop. She was turned in by one of the landlords of one of the buildings where she housed Jews. In light of her continuing religious resistance over the years, she was deemed an enemy of the state and sent to Ravensbrück Concentration Camp. In 1942, she was transferred to Auschwitz, where she was shot for conducting a layman's mass on Christmas day.

"I had to tell you this, you see? In case I die," Eve said to the nuns.

But before they could answer, the curtain flew open and the doctor barked, "What's the holdup? Let's go!"

Sisters Mary and Elizabeth jumped and snapped toward him.

"Calm yourself, Doctor," Sister Elizabeth said with uncharacteristic hostility. "This is a human being here."

And gently and carefully, she and Sister Mary pushed Eve's bed through the curtain and along the hall to X-ray.

XXI

When Eve came to, she was in pain. Through the drugged haze on her eyeballs, she could see a black nurse staring at her from the end of the bed. The woman looked angry.

"Hi," Eve mumbled.

"Uh huh," the nurse replied.

"Can I have some painkillers?" Eve asked. Her voice sounded slurry to her but it worked. She felt relieved. She was alive. She was all right.

"I'm checking the I.V., then it is my lunch."

The nurse had a West Indian accent. She spoke with such cruel ferocity and dismissiveness that it shocked Eve. There was a definite air of don't-provoke-me-or-I'll-savage-you coming out of the woman, as if Eve, in her broken and helpless state, were some kind of threat.

"Can I get them myself?"

Eve stifled what anger had managed to rise through the chaos of emotions she was feeling. This woman was a nurse. Just don't ask her to behave like one.

"Down the hall at the nurses' station," the woman hissed and left the room.

From out in the corridor, a thousand noises mingled and meshed. Beeps and bells, voices and loudspeaker announcements, crashes of metal, squeaks of wheels, human moans, and the occasional cries and screams.

A stab of pain caused Eve to look down at her forearm. There was no cast. The doctor had put the arm back together from the inside with pins and screws. Her forearm sat in a sling, purple and puffy, sadly limp. She examined it, prodding it with her finger, grateful to know that it had feeling, and then she realized: the tattoo was gone—in its stead, a neat row of suturing staples. Eva's lifeline to earth had been severed, her memory imprisoned by a newfangled barbed-wire fence.

Eva, Eve sobbed, Eva, Eva. I'm one of those who didn't resist. Forgive me. Eva.

But Eva was gone and Eve was all alone and in pain.

After a time, Eve decided to get up. She had to go to the nurses' station to get painkillers. She held one hand to the back of her head, and with great effort, pulled herself up. Her neck was so badly sprained, it was like a noodle. She moved her legs off the bed and set her feet on the floor. She stood up, steadying her body with her good arm, and couldn't believe the state of herself. She hurt all over. Every muscle in her body was bruised. But she was alive. Her life had been spared, but not Eva's.

She limped out the door of her room and stopped. There before her was a stained-glass window. It was the Virgin Mary cradling Jesus, and it was lovely. An old window, from the thirties, in beautiful, heart-thumping colors. Hitler promised them they'd be stained-glass windows and he couldn't keep his hands out of their underpants. It was heaven.

What? she asked herself. The women. Stained-glass windows, that's how he got them—stained-glass windows.

"Evie?"

She looked up and it was Charles César. He ws holding out a glass of water to her and two white pills. Her bruised condition obviously shocked him, but he was covering, sweetly brusque.

"What's this?" she asked, taking the pills and the water.

"Painkiller," he answered, surveying her, worried.

With his freed hands, he gently patted down her arms and legs, his own body search to make sure she was all right.

"Thank you for bringing this. How did you know?" The relief flowed out of her eyes. Her lower lip trembled.

"I know everything," he whispered, straightening up.

"Oh Charlie." She collapsed against him, melting into his chest. Her tears made water stains on his lovely silk tie. He clasped her to him and his sweet smell and his soft hair against her cheek calmed her.

"I leave you for a few weeks and look what happens," he murmured into her neck. "For God's sake," he blurted, losing control, weeping now, "are you all right? Are you sure?"

"I love you," she rasped. "Please forgive me. Please forgive me."

"I forgive you," he managed, "I forgive everybody. Come." He cradled her shoulders and led her back to the bed. Like the most loving father in the world, he placed her on it, laying her down, arranging her legs, gazing at her through his anguished wise eyes.

She stared up at him. "I saw you as—"

"A Jew?" he finished.

"A Jew in quotes," she amended.

"As soon as it became real. I told you."

"There's anti-Semitism in me," she said quickly. "I didn't know that. You don't want that."

"I'm used to it," he said sadly. "I chose it. It's in me too." Their eyes met mournfully through their tears.

"Look," she showed him. "The tattoo's gone. Penance."

"I'm one of those who didn't resist." A terrible sob escaped her heart. She bowed her head in shame.

"Oh, no, Eve," he comforted. "That isn't true."

"Can God forgive us for our sins?" she asked. "Will he?"

"God is love," he said softly, and he loosened his tie and unbuttoned his shirt, and took off his beautiful suit and dropped it in a heap on the floor.

"Open your legs," he whispered. And he climbed over her, setting his hands on either side of her body, keeping himself above her, careful not to rest his weight on any part of her. The crucifix he wore around his neck swung against his collarbone, and as the little Jesus dangled before her, she gazed into his tiny eyes.

"Help me," Charlie murmured. And with her hand guiding him, he pushed his way inside her and the feeling of being filled up eclipsed her pain. After a long, long time of loveliness, she whispered in his ear, "I'm afraid if I come I'll die."

"Me too," he whispered back.

XXII

The day after Eve came home from the hospital, Nelson Mandela was released from Victor Verster prison farm. She was propped up on the couch in the living area watching the twenty-four-hour news station with Mingus, the cat, snuggled in next to her. She'd spent two weeks in the hospital and her bruises had begun to subside. Her neck was still floppy and she felt fragile, but the bone in her arm was healing nicely. The external skin looked almost as it had before the accident except for a neat white seam, like a thick stroke of White-Out, where the tattoo had been.

On TV, the cameras switched back and forth between the gates of the prison and a stadium near Johannesburg where thousands of black South Africans were awaiting Mandela's arrival. Twenty-five years in prison, Eve thought, for his beliefs. He went to prison when he was around forty. Well, she thought, that can happen.

The excitement and anticipation of Mandela's release was expressed in the faces of everyone on the screen. Eve felt the joy rising inside her. It was another great day in the outer world. Another planetary shoe was about to drop. She thanked God she was alive.

After she and Charlie had made up in the hospital, it became an obsession with her to find Eva. She didn't know if she'd be retattooed and continue her narrative history. She was still smarting from the shock of her own ugliness, from the assault of her inner devils. She just didn't know if she was worthy. But she had to find Eva.

From her hospital bed, Eve had called the Yiddish Scientific Institute and they had told her that the identity and circumstances of 500123 could be found only in the archives at Auschwitz. She called a filmmaker friend, a man who, oddly enough, worked with Louise Kowalski, and he put her in touch with a student in Krakow whom Eve hired to go to Auschwitz and comb through the archives. Any day now the call would come, informing her about Eva.

But the telephone, Eve thought, was the worst instrument of communication ever invented. She had come to despise it. She had gotten only one call while in the hospital. The phone rang and a man's voice said, "Eve Flick?"

"Yes," she answered.

"My name is Rabbi Tassin. I was a friend of your Uncle Jim's. He took his life sometime yesterday. He's gone."

It seemed her Uncle Jim had committed suicide. Pills, it was, or powders. The lesions had begun to sprout deep in his throat. He hadn't told her that. She guessed he couldn't. She saw herself on that dusty Nogales side street, Jim with a row of staples across his mouth. They found him on his knees, Rabbi Tassin told her, in a praying position, a rosary clasped in his hands. He left a note for the men from the morgue, saying that he had AIDS, warning them to be careful.

She had gone to the chapel in the hospital to pray for her Uncle Jim's soul. She prayed there was a special place in heaven for those who died of AIDS. And she prayed there was a special place in hell for those who failed to resist.

On TV, coverage was suspended while the announcer gave the latest news. German reunification was proceeding apace. The American president had made an attempt to establish a consultancy of the conquering allies, but it had fizzled quickly.

Reunification was a fait accompli now and a united Germany, it was predicted, would be the strongest power in the European economic community.

Well, Eve thought, the world had just accepted it now, done with the past or weary with problems like the Soviet Union. People had decided to trust, which was not a bad thing. Sometimes trusting did result in the trusted being trustworthy.

But it seemed to Eve that the Germans, like her own countrymen with Vietnam, had never really healed the wound Nazism had caused them. The postwar world, like the Nazis themselves, had dubbed the phenomenon racism, and in part it was. But it was Eve's observation that when racism was cited as a cause for aberration, it was, to a naturally racist world, all too pat and acceptable. It did not explain, she thought, as the coverage flipped back to Verster Prison, why South African whites entrusted the care of their babies to women they feared would murder them in their beds. It did not explain why German women accepted, under Hitler, their own criminalization, through a barrage of laws so invasive, they conflicted with every God's every wish for humanity.

On TV, a car drove up before the prison gates and Winnie Mandela got out. She was all dressed up and beaming. She was getting her man back after twenty-five years, Eve thought. Twenty-five years of that empty-shell-longing-for-a-nutmeat feeling that can drive a woman mad . . .

"What's 'appening?"

Charles César hurried into the room and sat down next to her on the couch. She sank into him and he stroked her hair, and together they stared at the screen. He had moved back in and their life together was back to being as idyllic as life can be with someone you love in New York City. Mingus settled himself on Charlie's lap. The cat was perpetually smiling now that the aura in his home was restored to equanimity.

Eve glanced over at her typewriter. It still sat out on the table for all to see. Maybe it meant some important change. Maybe it was just that she was too weak to carry it to the closet. Sometimes, reasons don't matter.

"He should be released any minute," Eve said to Charlie and kissed him. "What a period this has been. So many things we'd thought we'd never see. My fortieth birthday. Yours." She pointed to the screen. "Theirs."

On TV, the president of South Africa was giving a speech in parliament, trying to calm the whites. The picture switched to a right-wing demonstration near the prison. The right-wingers were screaming and waving Nazi flags.

"Apartheid was enacted about forty years ago," she said.

Forty years, she thought. Again. That explosive time.

She looked up at Charlie. An image flashed in her mind. Charlie, waiting one Christmas on the steps of St. Patrick's Cathedral. His cheeks were as red as human hearts, his lovely hair was white with snow. In his long, skirted coat, he smiled that slow, warm smile and she wanted to confess to him. She was driven to confess to him.

"Look," he said.

On the screen, Mandela was emerging from the prison. His sweet, childlike face creased with pleasure and he waved. Eve and Charlie rocked with delight.

"Can it be?" Eve asked. "Can it be the world will be at peace? Can that be possible?"

"I have come to believe that anything is possible," Charlie replied.

Eve took his hand and caressed it.

Mandela and Winnie were escorted to the car. They got into it and were driven off.

"Do you think they'll have sex later?" Eve asked.

"Of course," Charlie said, "if he can."

They both glanced at her forearm, remembering what had happened to them before the accident.

The cameras switched to the stadium, to the thousands waiting.

"He promised them they'd be stained-glass windows and he couldn't keep his hands out of their underpants," Eve said.

"What?" Charlie asked.

"Hitler. I was thinking about Hitler and the women."

"Did you figure out how he got them to dump Christ?"

"Structure, I think. The structure of Nazism as he presented it was indistinguishable from the structure of Christianity. It promised an ascendancy through the glory of the Thousand Year Reich. The path to that ascendancy was purity, the purity of the race. He was the Christ figure. It was all so familiar to them, and their promised position in it so much more powerful than they could imagine—it was a bargain they couldn't refuse. I think it was a while before they realized they'd dumped Christ. Hitler was darling while he was dating Germany. It was only after they married that he started slapping her around."

"If only he'd gotten into art school." Charlie sighed.

The Mandelas had arrived at the stadium. The crowd was cheering. They were pushing to the front of the stage.

"And why didn't the women fear for themselves?" Charlie asked.

"They had already had it done to them," she replied. "Through the laws and the Euthanasia Program. By the time he started on the Jews, their women's hearts were hardened. I think mass breeding is the flip side of mass murder. Yin and yang."

"There is that theory that murder is outer-directed suicide," Charlie said.

"That's what I think, too. What the Germans let Hitler do to their society in the name of glory and purity was a suicidal act. Then they turned and perpetrated the same crime on Jews and anyone else they could find.

"You know why they arrested Jehova's Witnesses?" she asked.

"Why?"

"They refused to dump Christ."

On the stadium stage, the microphone was acting up. Mandela was waiting for them to fix it.

"Before Christ, there was no concept of mercy. Did you know that?" Charlie asked Eve.

"Yes," she said with shame.

"Do you feel better now, about the Christian women?" He cuddled her into his body.

"Well, you know," she said, "women always have to figure out how to be pure and still have sex. It was all going to be made clear for them by this fabulous guy whom they adored and trusted. They gave him their freedom in return for the clarity. But he conned them. They have to face it. We all do. It's a terribly old story. To which the moral is: Read a man's book before you marry him."

The microphone was fixed. Mandela walked up to it and began to speak. He spoke about freedom and how precious it is. He spoke about violence and said he would prefer not to use it but would if he had to. He spoke about the fight ahead of them, the battle against apartheid and how they would have to be strong. He thanked the Communists for their help in the lean times. And then he ended by saying something Eve had never heard a leader say in her lifetime. He said, "It is a cause for which I am prepared to die."

"My God," said Eve. "Do you think you'd have to be closeted away for twenty-five years to say those words and mean them?"

"During World War Two people said those words," Charlie said sadly, "some people."

Eve kissed his cheek.

They both focused on the screen where thousands of modern slaves were screaming for joy. *Amandla!* Freedom.

"I think freedom is the most precious thing in life." She looked up at Charlie. "Do you?"

He didn't reply. He seemed to be thinking about something else. He muted the sound. On TV they were now showing old footage of Mandela before he went to prison, when he was 184   around forty.

"Charlie," Eve asked, "did you like the Elie Wiesel piece I sent you? Did it help?"

"Intellectually," he replied. "It reminded me of the day I found out my parents were catchers."

"When was that?" Eve was treading carefully. It was the first time he had ever spoken about his childhood.

"At the *lycée*. At school. A new boy came that semester. A great athlete, so good that he was made captain of the soccer team. Jacques Levi was his name. I really admired him. He could run like a cheetah. Beautiful to watch.

"I was good, too. I was a forward on the team. But one day I came to school and checked the bulletin board and found that I was no longer on the team roster. I thought it must be a mistake, so I went out onto the playing field where the team was gathered with Jacques.

I began to ask him about it and he said, "We don't want you on the team. Your parents were collaborators. They were catchers. Because of your parents, my father is dead."

"Many things made sense to me in that moment. Puzzling things my parents had said and done over the years. I knew Jacques was telling the truth. So, I simply turned and walked away across the playing field and out into the countryside. In my pocket I had some francs with which I was to pay for the team uniform. I walked to a nearby farm and I paid them to a farmgirl who I fucked in the hayloft until I thought my anger was spent." He paused here. It was difficult for him to say what he was going to say. "But it wasn't," he added finally. "I went on fucking it out for twenty-five more years until you got the tattoo and I could fuck no more. I think I used my dick like a pole to keep distance between me and women. I never fucked Louise Kowalski, Eve."

Eve looked at him. A fire reignited in her heart. She was only human after all.

"You didn't?"

"No. We did other things, but not that. She didn't want to be penetrated until her wedding night—"

Eve hooted.

"And that was fine with me. At that point, I didn't care if I ever fucked again."

"Charlie," Eve said joyously. "Charlie!" And she rolled over on him and kissed him.

"Look at you," he said, ruffling her hair, gazing up into her eyes, "you're so jealous."

The phone rang and they both said simultaneously, "Shit!"

Eve reached for it and said curtly into the receiver, "Yes? Oh. It's Poland," she said to Charles César. "Hang on. Let me change to the other phone. Hang it up for me, will you?"

And she left the room.

About fifteen minutes later, Eve came back into the living room carrying the photo of the woman she called Eva. She set it up on the coffee table so both she and Charlie could see it, then she sat down on the couch. She felt odd, a combination of peace and sadness such as one feels on the day one comes home from a long and satisfying trip.

"I'm going to tell you about her now," she said, "using the facts I've been given, just the way I used to tell one of my tales."

"Okay," he said. "I'm ready."

Eva's name was Leni Essen, Eve said. She was forty years old at the time of her arrest in November of 1944 and she lived in Cologne. Leni was a working-class housewife. She had three children, a daughter, Gretel, age twenty, and two twin sons, Klaus and Rupert, age fifteen. Leni's husband, Martin, a bricklayer, died in the battle of Stalingrad in 1943. And she was just as glad. In her life she had had fourteen miscarriages, thanks to the help of her doctor. The minute she heard of her husband's death, she got herself sterilized.

Leni considered herself a Nazi.

Charles César looked at Eve questioningly.

Leni wanted to keep up, Eve went on. It was the most
important thing to her next to her family. She and Martin had

been born dirt poor. She was determined to have better for her children. When her women friends told her better was what the Führer promised, she immediately went over to his side.

Leni was bored by politics. She didn't read the papers. But she wanted all the things the Nazis offered and, with little difficulty, she followed the rules. She delivered three children before her husband left for war. Both her and Martin's families were, as it happened, racially pure. Nobody drank. Nobody was odd. Before the Nazis came to power, she had thought of her lot as terribly tedious. Now she was proud.

Leni was not truly religious. She went to church because it was done. She joined the Protestant Women's group in hopes of meeting a better class of people. In '36 when the Nazis took over her church group, some protested, but not Leni. She didn't want to make waves, and when she saw that some of the more powerful women embraced the Nazis with gusto, she followed suit. She didn't understand Nazi ideology nor did she care. But she did believe in being pure and proper and in not giving the neighbors reason to gossip. More than anything, Leni wanted to be treated like a lady while not being accused of giving herself airs. It was a difficult row to hoe.

When the war began, Leni had to go to work in a bullet-casing factory. She felt factory work was a step back from the proud position she had assumed as a Nazi housewife and mother. But when the Nazis proclaimed she was a heroine doing war work for the Fatherland, she swallowed her pride and spoke amusedly of the difficulties of washing the casing oil off her skin.

Leni was very pretty, younger-looking than her forty years, but she was terribly lonely. Her daughter, Gretel, had been conscripted by the Nazis for war work in Düsseldorf and so was never at home. Her only personal joy was her twin sons, whom she adored and for whom she had the highest aspirations. She sent them both to Hitler Youth and she hoped one day they would rise very high up in the SS.

As the war had escalated, Leni's life, like that of the other working-class women in her downtrodden neighborhood, had 187 become increasingly difficult. Due to the Allied bombings, her street was a shambles of rubble, her nerves were shot, and food was becoming scarce. By the end of '43, when her twins left school, people were beginning to whisper that the Nazis were losing the war. In public, she vehemently denied this possibility, but in her heart she was afraid. It was getting harder and harder to keep up appearances. As if this all weren't enough, her sons, Klaus and Rupert, began to rebel.

She found out about it in February of '44, when they came out of their room wearing very odd outfits and announced that they were no longer in Hitler Youth. They were wearing checked shirts, short, dark trousers, white socks, dark caps, and jackets. Little metal sprigs of edelweiss flowers were pinned to their lapels.

"We hate Hitler Youth. We are Edelweiss Pirates now, Mother. Sworn to avenge those little creeps."

Leni was stunned. "I will not permit it!" she raised her voice. "We have our reputation to think of. We are not street trash. I will not permit it!"

"Try and stop us!" they shouted back and swaggered from the room.

Leni was horrified. Klaus and Rupert had joined a gang. She had heard other mothers complaining about these Edelweiss Pirates. Boys and girls banding together, loitering in the parks, doing God knows what, and perhaps worst of all, anti-Nazi.

Klaus and Rupert began hanging out by the canals. They stayed out late, and one night they came home bruised and bloody.

"What happened?" Leni demanded.

Klaus kept silent. "Nothing," Rupert mumbled.

"Tell me what happened now!" Leni stood in her nightgown, hands on her hips, the archetypal Mother.

"We got in a fight."

"Who with?"

Silence. The boys glanced at each other.

"I said, who with?"

"A Hitler Youth patrol," Klaus mumbled. Rupert glared at him.

Leni collapsed in a chair. "What are you doing?" she cried. "Why are you doing this to me?"

"It's not to you, Mother. You don't understand," said Rupert.

"No, it's you who don't understand. Through Hitler Youth you can become something. You can rise. You—" Here Leni broke into tears. "If only your father were here—" She broke down sobbing.

Klaus and Rupert rolled their eyes heavenward. "Don't, Mother," they said simultaneously. "Try and understand: we're different from you. We want different things than you."

But Leni was inconsolable. She bathed their wounds and then went to bed, but she couldn't sleep. She felt she was losing control. When at 3 a.m. the air-raid alert sounded and she went and got the boys to go down to the shelter, she was glad. She spent the rest of the night between them, holding them close, while the sounds of destruction raged outside.

Leni put the episode out of her mind. Actually, as daylight bombing was stepped up, she couldn't think about much else. Her house was still standing, but the two on either side had collapsed and much of what free time she had was consumed with relief work for her neighbors. She couldn't keep track of the boys. She worried about them constantly but not because of the gang. She feared bombs would kill them or falling masonry or madmen lurking in the ruins.

For their part, Klaus and Rupert had decided to lie low. They put on their Pirate outfits now only after leaving the house. They sneaked behind the rubble next door and hurriedly dressed. Then they met up with their friends.

Leni thought they had seen the light until about two months later when the Gestapo came to her door.

"Heil Hitler! Won't you come in?" Leni said graciously,

though her heart was pounding. "Whatever can I do for you?"

The Gestapo man was curt. "You have two sons, Klaus and Rupert Essen?"

"Yes. Is anything wrong?"

"They are part of the gang, Edelweiss Pirates?"

"Oh no," Leni lied. "Oh no. I would know if they were. I'm their mother."

The Gestapo man stared at her.

"They are suspected of defacing subway walls," he continued. "Slogans such as 'Down With Hitler, 'The Military High Command Is Lying,' 'Down With Nazi Brutality.' "

Leni's mouth dropped open. "Oh, my God," she said and then quickly, "Not my boys. Never my boys. There must be some mistake."

"This is treason, Frau Essen, be warned. Next time we will not be so lenient."

When Klaus and Rupert came home, Leni walked up to them and slapped them both across the face.

"The Gestapo was here," she managed through her rage. "In my home, accusing my family of treason! I am shamed. I am shamed to the bottom of my soul! How could you?! How could you be so ungrateful?! You are a disgrace to the Fatherland," she fumed. "Your father gave his life for the Reich."

The twins looked abashed at this.

She went on. "After all the Führer has done for us—"

"What has he done, Mother? Look around you!" Klaus shouted.

"We almost starved when you were babies," she hissed. "When the Führer came, we got work and food. We traveled! For the first time in our lives we got out of this wretched neighborhood. The Führer gave us those special package tours. Remember our trip in 'thirty-six? That hotel? You liked that well enough!" She rushed to the dresser, opened a drawer, and pulled out a photo album. "See! You're smiling here! See!"

She shoved the album in their faces. They lowered their
heads sullenly.

"We went to the theater and films. Before the Führer we had nothing. We were poor trash, doomed to oblivion. Do you think I would ever have gone to the theater were it not for him?"

The boys were silent. Leni's rage was building now. She ran around the dining room pointing at objects. "This dinette set, designed by the Ministry of Housing, cheap enough for us to buy. Do you think a woman of my class would have had such a thing without the Nazis? Look at this beautiful sideboard. Look at it!"

The boys looked. The lines were simple and clean. The wood was light beige. The knobs on all the drawers were little brass heads of Adolf Hitler.

"My pride and joy! You must stop! You must stop, do you hear me!"

She sank into a chair with swastikas carved into its back and wept. "What will the neighbors say?" she burbled.

"What neighbors, Mother? The whole street's in ruins." Klaus knelt down before her.

"We're tired of it, Mother. We don't want to march in neat rows and sing stupid songs. We don't want to be barked at and screamed at and kept on leashes like dogs. We're young. We want to have love and adventure and laugh. Your world is prison, Mother."

"Prison is where you'll end up if you don't listen to me—" Leni began but she never got to finish because the air-raid alert sounded and the boys grabbed her and took her, running, to the shelter, where they deposited her with the neighbors and then retreated to a corner where other members of the Pirates were huddled.

After that, Leni's relationship with the boys grew distant. They spoke to each other in one-syllable phrases and she ceased asking them what they were doing. Finally, when she could stand the loneliness no longer, she poured out her heart to her neighbor, Marta.

"It's just adolescence, Leni," Marta consoled. "It will pass. My boys were impossible. I never thought I'd get through it.

And with all that's going on—" Marta gestured around her. They were standing outside the shelter. There was rubble everywhere. Smoke from burning houses in the next district filled the air. Their clothes were faded and dirty from lack of washing water. They both looked like hell.

"I just wanted a better life, you know?" Leni said wearily.

"The Führer says it will get better."

"Heil Hitler." Leni nodded and they threaded their way through debris back to their street.

In the autumn of '44, Leni began dating an SS man named Maximilian. He was assigned to her district to protect the populace from German army deserters, runaway forced laborers, and escaped concentration camp prisoners who, he told her, were living in the bombed-out buildings. Further, he said, he was rooting out an underground group aiding and abetting these criminals. He made Leni feel safe. Klaus and Rupert were rarely home now, only returning to bring her food and various items they'd scammed from the rubble. The day the chief of the Gestapo in Cologne was assassinated, and the district was in an uproar, it was Maximilian who came by to see if she was all right. House searches were being conducted and he himself conducted hers, making sure it was done neatly and with dignity. In the twins' room, she found a pamphlet dropped by the Allied bombers. She stuffed it in her bra. The search turned up nothing.

For two weeks after the assassination, she did not hear from Klaus or Rupert. She was terrified. She roamed the parks and canals looking for gang members but to no avail. Finally, she went down to Gestapo headquarters wearing her swastika lapel pin and inquired. She got no information. At night she sat in the kitchen with a candle burning, waiting, but the boys never came.

One afternoon in November of 1944, Marta came running into Leni's house, screaming.

"Leni! Leni!" Marta ran into the kitchen where Leni had fallen asleep in a chair. Leni bolted to her feet.

"Leni, oh, Leni!" Marta was out of breath. In her eyes lurked terror broken with sorrow. She was trying to find the words.

"They're . . . They're hanging Klaus and Rupert!"

Leni grabbed the first weapon she could find, a butcher knife. She and Marta ran through the rubble, past fires and corpses, through packs of dogs, until they reached an open square. There Leni stopped. On a makeshift scaffold, twelve adolescent boys she recognized were hanging by their necks, the last two, Klaus and Rupert, the life gone out of them, their eyes rolled up in their heads, their mouths slacked open, already dead. A scream came out of Leni's mouth so wild that the gathered crowd turned as one to look at her. She lunged with the butcher knife and stabbed the first SS man she saw. It happened to be Maximilian, who instantly shot her in both legs.

Leni was arrested and taken to prison. There her wounds were attended to for some reason, possibly because Max's wound was only superficial. She was sent to a series of concentration camps, ending up at Auschwitz, where, because of the chaos there in '44, she was tattooed by mistake.

She was murdered by a capo in a fight over some bread a week before liberation.

"That was five-oh-oh-one-two-three, Charlie. That was Eva."

They both stared at her picture. Now they understood the defiance in her stance, the hatred in her eyes. It was different than either of them had imagined, 180 degrees different.

On TV, the station had cut Mandela's speech into sound bytes. "It is a cause for which I am willing to die," he said between commercial spots and snippets of inane commentary.

"Eve, in the hospital?" Charlie said.

Eve looked over at him.

"It was the first time I fucked without anger, the first time I ever felt love."

She reached for his hand. "Do you know what made me get the tattoo?"

He looked at her.

"I found this."

She took from her pocket the item she had found in his closet when he moved back in, the item he had secreted in his suitcase the day he left.

"And when I found it, I knew you must be Jewish. And if you were Jewish and we were living in Nazi Germany, I'd be barred by law from loving you."

She laid the piece of cloth across his lap. They both stared down at it.

"It's Ben's," he said, naming a filmmaker friend. "He brought it over to show me and forgot it. He bought it last year from a Neo-Nazi booth in a flea market in Berlin. I meant to show it to you but then you got the tattoo—I don't know why I kept it. I don't know why."

"You turned forty," she said.

He smiled at her and once more he was her Vatican cardinal, once more he was her prince of the church.

"I see now," she said, getting up and going to sit by him. "I see what Mr. Schlaren didn't want to tell me."

"What?" asked Charlie. He wasn't listening. He was looking down at the piece of cloth on his lap.

She took one end and he took the other, and together, they picked it up and examined it. It was a Star of David armband from the Nazi era. Homemade, obviously, by someone's wife or mother. The big yellow star was carefully positioned in the middle of a strip of white material and painstakingly sewn with hundreds of handmade little stitches. The cloth was old and threadbare as they handled it. The yellow of the star was faded now. A weak yellow, as weak as a dying sun.